Elena Kincaid, Maia Dylan, and Sarah Marsh

EVERNIGHT PUBLISHING ®

www.evernightpublishing.com

Editor: Karyn White

Cover Artist: Jay Aheer

ISBN: 978-1-77339-370-4

Elena Kincaid, Maia Dylan, and Sarah Marsh

DEDICATION

We would like to dedicate this book to all of our fantastic and amazingly supportive street team members in our Sinfully More Erotic group! This entire series was born right there in a contest. Our winners Avril, Julie, and Tami chose the building blocks for the story and we couldn't be happier with how our first trio came out. Thank you all for the inspiration!

Elena Kincaid, Maia Dylan, and Sarah Marsh

CHASING FAETE

Beyond the Veil, 1

Elena Kincaid, Maia Dylan, and Sarah Marsh

Copyright © 2016

Chapter One

"Fuck, fuck, fuckity fuck," Erica half growled, half moaned as she entered an alleyway she had stumbled down, only to find that she reached a dead end. And wasn't that just painfully ironic, she mused, considering she might potentially be about to meet her own *dead end. Ha!*

Even with the threat of certain death hanging over her, she still thought herself quite funny.

It was late at night, and she could hear the steady thump of rock music coming from inside the bar she had just passed. The air was thick with the smell of stale beer, cigarette smoke, and urine. She glanced around the dark alley in a panic trying to find a means of escape, but could find none. On one side of her, she saw a side entrance to the bar, but unfortunately, there was no handle on this side of the door, only a lock that required a key.

She pressed herself against the brick wall on the darkest side of the alley, biting back a moan as the move put pressure on her wounds. Erica took three deep breaths, releasing them slowly. She only had about two or three minutes before Alefric's guards found her. She was a healer with no equal, and needed to heal herself enough to fight back or this was going to be one hell of a short escape story … and one that no one would hear.

Closing her eyes, Erica called upon her inner healing light, sending it deep into her own body. She felt the warmth of it flooding through her, seeking out her injuries. She ignored most of them, and directed it to the two stab wounds on her right side, hoping to stem the blood loss enough to give her a fighting chance.

A noise coming from the front of the alley had her coming fully back to herself and her eyes snapping open. She had managed to close off one wound, but the other still bled sluggishly. She wasn't losing as much blood as she had been before, but too much for her to hope to last too long.

"Come on out now, Erica," a man's voice called out, and Erica shivered in dread. She recognized that voice. "Why don't you just come on out, and we'll take you back, all nice and peaceful like."

Kheelan. He was the captain of Alefric's guards, and her chances of getting out of this alive had dropped from around sixty-five percent to closer to ten. He stood a foot taller than her five foot four, was lean but muscular. His long black hair was tied back with a leather tie, and Erica believed he did that so the scar that ran from the corner of his left eye to his jawline was clearly visible. He was as ruthless as he was evil, and he took a sadistic kind of pleasure in seeing her in pain. Erica had promised herself that if she ever made it out of the Elven realm she would rather die before she would allow herself to be returned. Kheelan was a large part of the reason for her making that decision.

Erica fought back the tears and drew her anger and her rage around her like a cloak, a trick she had learned from her mother. She pushed her fear and her pain behind the cloak. Lifting her head and squaring her shoulders, she pushed off from the wall and stepped out into the alley, not stopping until she stood in the pale glow of the murky "Exit Only" sign above the door to the bar.

She stood proud and tall, no one would suspect she was as hurt as she was. "Hey Khee, aren't you sick of doing all of Alefric's dirty work? Or do you just like being his bitch?"

She knew she'd scored a direct hit to his ego when Kheelan's dark eyes flickered red. "I believe you still hold that position, *Ittee*." Kheelan spat the Elven word for a whore at her, and Erica had to force herself not to laugh. She had been with only two men in her entire life. Kheelan on the other hand had fucked his way through half the ranks of the Elven guard, male and female, and *she* was the whore?

Erica tensed when three more of his guard stepped into the alley behind Kheelan. "You know, Alefric was gravely concerned when he was told you had left the Elven realm. I have never seen him so distressed," Kheelan said with a smile, but, because the man had never smiled once in his life before, it came across as more of a snarl.

"Firstly, let's call it what it was—an *escape*," Erica said. "I didn't just leave. You make it sound like I was simply over for tea and biscuits and left without saying thanks. I had been held captive in that realm … in my own home, Kheelan. I can assure you, I certainly wasn't going to fucking thank you for the beatings and the torture."

Kheelan's face slid into its usual leer. "But, princess, you took them so well! When you would make me work for your cries and screams, *mmmm*." Erica had to swallow the bile that rose in her throat at the perverse sound of pleasure the sadistic bastard made. "I lived for those days."

They had kept her shackled in a small bedroom located near the dungeons. Alefric claimed that he was being hospitable by not throwing her in a dirty cell, though sometimes he liked to remind her of his *hospitality* by isolating her in those cells for days if she was being particularly unruly. The shackles prevented her from not only using some of her unique powers to fight back or even to heal herself.

Determined not to show any weakness, Erica shrugged. "Well, that seems only fair. I lived for the days, and let's be honest there were a lot of them, when you disappointed your King, and he had you beaten on the stairs of the palace."

Kheelan's eyes now blazed red, and Erica grinned knowing that she had won this round. But, because she was a woman who never understood the concept of quitting while she was ahead, she decided to add one final little verbal jab.

"I have been meaning to tell you this for a while now, Kheelan. I know you were jealous of all the times Alefric turned his unwanted attentions on me, but take it from a woman who knows, there's not a lot there to covet if you know what I mean." Erica waggled her pinky finger in the air to drive her point home and just in case he was too daft to understand her meaning. She had never actually seen Alefric naked, but Kheelan didn't need to know that. Kheelan definitely had, and by the angry look he presently gave her, she knew she had hit the nail on the head.

"Shut your mouth, bitch! How dare you talk of our King like that! He—"

"He is no King of mine!" Erica yelled, losing hold of her anger for the first time. "He is nothing more to me than someone I want to *kill.* He murdered my family, destroyed our kingdom, and he deserves to die slowly and very painfully. Now, you came here to do a job, asshole, so why don't you stop with the endless posturing, and inane fucking pissing contests, and just come at me."

Erica drew the curved blade of her kind from the sheath she wore behind her back, charged it with energy, making it glow an eerie blue, and slid with practiced ease into her battle stance. Her right foot slid back, leaving her to balance on the balls of her feet. She held her sword in a two handed grip and dropped her weight back on her right leg.

Live or die this night, she took comfort in the fact that she would be free. Ignoring the battle cry of the three men who now charged her, she prepared to either meet death face to face or be the harbinger of it.

Chapter Two

Leo could barely stop himself from growling at the drunk humans who bumped and pushed their way through the crowded bar. He looked back at his brother Ben and was not surprised to see him flirting with some woman while they were supposed to be hunting. They were Enforcers for their wolf pack, and it was their job to protect their territory. They'd been hitting bars all over town, trying to catch a scent. Gabe, the Alpha of their pack, had tasked them with finding out why a sudden influx of Fae were coming into their town during the last six months, and pack members had been reporting seeing and feeling them in even more unusual numbers for the past week. The Fae were known opportunists when it came to picking up strays in bars, so that was where Leo and Ben decided to start their search.

"Ben, stop fucking around," Leo growled low enough so the humans wouldn't be able to hear him over the rhythmic booming of the music. "We're working, not looking to get laid."

"Don't be so grumpy, brother. Maybe if you actually got laid once in a while you wouldn't be such a dick all of the time," Ben replied, still smiling at the exceedingly drunk blonde with fake tits in front of him.

Ben may have liked to joke a lot with his big brother, but Leo knew that it was to cover up his concern for Leo's ever changing moods. He also knew that the comic relief and playboy act were just to conceal his own pain. As the years went by, it seemed as if Leo grew less and less interested in the pleasures life had to offer, and just threw himself into his job of protecting the pack. Leo had stepped up to fill in the missing role of their parents after they had been killed, forcing him to grow up faster than his little brother. He hadn't even been on a real date in over three years. He may have fucked a few women here and there, but even that hadn't happened in a while. Everything just seemed unworthy of his time lately, even though wolves by nature were social creatures, and wolf shifters were no different. The way he kept to himself was a concern for the entire pack, but a feeling in his gut had told him something big was coming. Ben had expressed his guilt about having the chance to enjoy most of his childhood while his big brother took on a more paternal role, and he had also expressed on many occasions that it was time to let that role go and just be brothers again … equals.

Leo began to head in Ben's direction, resolved to pry him away from the blonde if he had to, but then he noticed his brother stop dead in his tracks.

"What is it, Ben?" Leo asked, approaching closer to his brother. "Do you have their scent?"

"It's not like any Fae scent that I've ever smelled before. Usually, they make me sneeze, but this—oh brother, this makes my wolf want to roll around in it."

That certainly got Leo's attention, and as he lifted his nose to hone in on the aroma, his wolf perked up and started turning circles in his head. His nostrils flared, and he inhaled deeper, smelling freshly turned soil and a summer wind. His feet automatically began to follow it to the back of the bar. Good gods, her scent was amazing. He knew it was a female that he was scenting because his wolf became rather insistent on that fact.

Claim her. She's ours! His wolf repeated in his mind, over and over again. Something else clawed at his senses, however. Another scent combined with the delectable mystery woman's. A tangy, metallic scent he knew all too well. Blood.

Ben must have picked up on it at the same time

because he took off like a shot toward the back door that led to the alley and threw the door open. Leo heard the sound of glass tumbling to the ground and breaking as the door knocked over boxes of empty beer bottles. Then the overwhelming scent of male Fae hit him square in the face as he and Ben burst into the alley. Just then, three Fae charged at a beautiful woman who expertly swung a large and elaborate curved blade.

Leo's wolf came to the surface so fast that he almost lost control and shifted fully—not something he wanted to do right in the heart of downtown Vancouver. The last thing their pack needed was a bunch of wolf sightings stirring up the local law enforcement. He kept the partial shift, however, to have access to his deadly claws. He saw Ben doing the same through his peripheral vision, and they both rushed forward into the fray to even the odds.

Between the delicious smell of the female and the fact that she was holding her own quite well with that blade against a male twice her size, he felt oddly turned on by the entire situation. It surprised him. He hadn't even noticed a female in months, let alone been motivated enough to get between her thighs, but this little pixie of a woman with her spiky black hair and her fierce attitude made his cock hard enough to leave a zipper imprint from his jeans. When the Fae he was fighting over-swung and left his right side open, Leo immediately took advantage and sank his claws deep into the male's neck, quickly pulling back and severing the artery. The Fae turned to ash before his body hit the ground, and Leo turned to see his brother finish the second male. The fact that the Fae just up and disintegrated in their realm when killed made watching them die creepy as hell.

One more threat to the woman remained. He and

Ben both advanced to where the female still sparred with the head goon. Leo could see that the woman had taken some damage. She had blood all along her side and lower abdomen along with a few long gashes on her arms. The long-haired male she fought with sported his own declarations of her obvious skill with a blade. She'd left him with a deep bleeding cut across his left cheek and several long marks on his chest.

It became clear to Leo though that from the amount of blood the beauty appeared to have lost, her energy was fading fast. As Leo and Ben advanced on the fighting pair, the Fae goon must have finally noticed them and that his comrades were now nothing more than dust stirring up in the wind. He lunged hard at the pixie one more time before he fled toward the street. Leo's wolf almost gave chase, and if not for the smell of blood in the air, he surely would have. His pixie … his *mate* was hurt, taking precedence over everything now.

Well, shit! His wolf had just deemed this pretty little pixie of a female his mate. He involuntarily took in a big gulp of air, inhaling more of her fragrance. Now that he stood closer to her, another scent permeated his nostrils and shocked the hell out of him. His little beauty was Fae herself.

This definitely complicates matters, Leo thought. Their Alpha was at war with the Fae King, and furthermore, if he wasn't mistaken by how adoringly his brother stared at the small woman in front of them, both Leo and Ben had just found their mate … and she was Fae.

He really had not seen *that* coming tonight when they'd set out on a routine mission.

Chapter Three

Impossible, Ben thought. *Wolves do not have Fae mates.* Nevertheless, his wolf, as of this moment, would accept no other. He saw fire mixed with panic in her eyes as she stared the two of them down, and yet an aura of pure courage surrounded her fear. Ben figured she was trying to discern whether he and Leo posed a threat. His heart thumped and melted, drunken blonde forgotten. He was actually quite disgusted with his behavior as of late and wondered what his mate would think of him for it … that was if she lived through all of her injuries.

Ben was about to let her know that she was safe when he noticed her eyes rolling back. Within seconds, her entire body went slack, and he and Leo both sprinted toward her, managing to catch her before she hit the concrete. They then gently laid her on the ground.

Blood. Oh, gods, there was so much blood! If she had been a wolf or a human even, he and Leo could heal her with their bite. Mates had the ability to do that, but the physiology of Fae was still foreign to his kind. He feared what his bite would do to her. Suddenly, a clawing, choking feeling in his gut took hold at the possibility of seeing her disintegrate before his eyes.

"Fuck that!" Ben spat. "Put pressure here so that she doesn't bleed out," he ordered his brother, going into full medic mode now. He sent up a thank you to the gods for his training, though he scarcely got to use it since being bumped up to Enforcer status.

"We'll get her to Corinne," Leo replied calmly, his tone belying the panic and barely suppressed rage clearly visible on his face.

That was his big brother though—calm and collected, always rational no matter the circumstance, and he did just make a very good call. Corinne was the only Fae his people trusted. She had sought out his Alpha when the wrongful Fae King stole the throne, and begged for his help. She then went into hiding and was under their pack's protection because if she was ever caught, her death would be far from swift and painless. The False King and his goons liked to make examples of traitors.

Still, despite assisting them, she had remained secretive about her kind, and he could understand this very well. In a time of war, it was hard to trust. How could she know the wolves would not use the Fae secrets against them when a rightful king was appointed? There existed just as much greed for power and corruption amongst the wolves as amongst the Fae. He just hoped that Corrine would help her fellow Fae. Since their little pixie had just fought with men wearing the Royal Guard emblem on their clothing, Ben concluded that she was more than likely no friend to the False King either.

They needed to get her stabilized before they could move her, however. While Leo put pressure on the large, gaping gash in her right side, Ben tried to staunch the bleeding from yet another deep wound in her stomach. He had seen the bastard stab her before he fled like a fucking coward. If they couldn't stabilize and move her quickly, she'd bleed out. Once again, the image of her turning into nothing more than ash assaulted him.

"M-move," their little pixie stuttered barely above a whisper, her eyes still closed.

"Shhh," Leo cooed. "It's going to be all right. My brother is going to stop the bleeding, and then we are going to take you somewhere safe."

"I d-don't want to … to—"

"Don't try to talk now," Ben commanded gently. "There's no need to overexert yourself." Trying to speak seemed to only cause her more pain.

"…to hurt you," she finished, finally opening her eyes. "P-please move."

"Hush now. Let me take care of—" Before Ben had a chance to calm her down again, he and Leo were thrown backward by a glowing ball of clear white light. He had never seen anything like it. Within minutes, a rosy color came rushing back onto their pixie's face. A few minutes more, and Ben watched with no little fascination as her wounds began to close, until there were no more wounds left to speak of. The only evidence that she had in fact been mortally wounded was the copious amount of blood—not fully dried—on her clothes and skin.

She sat up slowly, put her head in her hands, and let out a strangled sob. Just as quickly, she composed herself and looked up at Ben and Leo with her big, beautiful, blue tear-stained eyes. "Thank you. I would have died tonight if not for the two of you."

Leo lifted his hands slowly, a sign he meant to approach her without harm. She nodded. Leo stood and walked over to their pixie, and Ben followed suit. They then both knelt beside her, after which Ben asked, "Are you still in any pain, pixie?"

Their pixie chuckled, followed by a wince. Despite not having any visible wounds, she was clearly still in pain. "Although being called a pixie is amusing, you may call me Erica. And to answer your question, I feel a little sore, but hey, that beats still being sliced open, right?"

Ben was not amused at her nonchalance at nearly dying. "Can all Fae do that?" he asked, regretting it right after. Erica's guard, which she had lowered for them, immediately went back up. "I'm sorry. I'm not trying to pump you for information. I am just curious."

And I want to make sure that the bastards who want to harm you will die when I mortally wound them and they turn to fucking ash! He also held back the fact that she was a mate to him and Leo, at least for now, until he could ascertain what her reaction might be.

Erica cocked her head to the side and looked him in the eye. She then bestowed her penetrating gaze on Leo before locking eyes with him again. "No ... not all of us can do what I can. I'm ... a little different."

Ben sensed that for now the subject was closed and let it be. Fae or not, she was their mate. She would have to trust them eventually, but he and his brother would have to let it be on her own terms. He found that he already trusted her. He might not always be as intuitive as his big brother, but his gut told him that she was pure goodness, while his wolf growled for him to strip her, fuck her until she knew who she belonged to, and then track down every single bastard who had ever tried to hurt her, and kill them all.

Calm the fuck down! he mentally chided his wolf. He also saw Leo's lips twitch and could sense that his brother's wolf was misbehaving just as much. "We need to get you somewhere safe in case the False King decides to send more goons." Ben stood, holding out his hand for Erica to take.

"False King, eh?" Erica nodded her approval. "That's exactly what Alefric is." She reached up and took his hand, but nearly lost her footing on the way up.

"Whoa, easy there," Ben said catching her in his arms. "You're still a little weak. Let me carry you."

"I am not going to be carried around by two overgrown wolves when my feet work perfectly fine. Just give me a minute, will you? It's not every day a girl gets nearly stabbed to death, and then lives to fight another day."

Ben did not like the sound of hearing his woman fighting another day and neither did his wolf. He and Leo would be taking care of the fighting from here on out. "As much as it amuses me to be called an overgrown wolf, I'm Ben, and this here big guy is my brother, Leo."

Leo chuckled, and Ben was glad to see a ghost of a smile from Erica.

"My truck is parked a block away," Leo stated.

Ben scooped Erica up in his arms. The look of shock on her face was priceless, but she did not have time to protest as he and Leo immediately high tailed it out of the alley toward the car. "I am very glad to hear that your feet are working, by the way," he informed her. "I look forward to your demonstration later."

Erica opened her mouth to say something but shut it just as quickly. She was definitely going to be a stubborn one. He could already sense it, and his excitement bubbled over. She was safe in his arms. That's what mattered. He and Leo would soon claim her, and as she had pointed out, they were all alive to fight another day.

Chapter Four

"So this is home for you two, huh?" Erica asked as she sat down on the surprisingly comfy if overly large leather couch. The apartment the two shifters brought her to was located at the west end of Vancouver. It was large, mostly all open plan, with lots of windows allowing for spectacular views of downtown, and a glimpse or two of English Bay.

Ben grinned as he placed a tall glass of water on the coffee table in front of her and sat down beside her. "We have a couple of places we call home, but this place is available to anyone in the pack to stay when they are needed in the city. Leo and I prefer the place we have up near Lynn Creek. A wolf's gotta have a place to roam and howl at the moon, babe."

Erica reached for the glass and lifted it, a move that had more to do with filling in the silence than it did with thirst. "Are you part of the pack here in Vancouver or one of the smaller packs from the outlying areas?"

"Why do you want to know?" Leo asked from his position by the windows opposite the couch. Of the two brothers, he was the more introverted and serious. "Have you been sent here by your *King* to find out more about the packs in this area? What's your mission here? Get as much information as possible to help him win this damn war? Because I gotta tell you, pixie, if that's your plan, you're shit outta luck."

Erica felt her anger start to build, and she took a slow sip of water, mentally counting to ten in an effort to calm herself down. She got as far as eight before she could hold her tongue no more. "Have you had this problem with your short term memory for long? Or perhaps you've suffered a severe head injury lately?" Erica reveled in Leo's immediate confusion. "Not that I owe you any type of explanation, but I will say this. Have you forgotten that little scene you encountered outside that bar tonight? If so, let me sum up for you. They were the King's guards, and they were sent here to either return me to the Elven realm or kill me. The long-haired fucker I was tangling with, the one that made off like a damn thief in the night, is the Captain of his guard."

Ben leaned forward from his place beside her, making a *T* out of his hands. "Time out, guys. Why don't we take a few moments and—"

Erica interrupted, completely ignoring Ben attempt at peacekeeping, her eyes never leaving Leo's as she impatiently asked, "Did you think that the fact he was trying his best to slam his sword right through my abdomen was part of his performance appraisal process? Oh goddess, can you use your brain for a moment and try to think before you accuse me of any kind of wrongdoing or espionage? You yourself called Alefric the 'False King', which tells me that you must have Fae friends in this realm who have told you about that prick and the atrocities he is responsible for against *my* people."

Leo made a sound of pure frustration as he ran his hands through his hair. Erica had to fight her physical reaction to the man as the muscles in his arms rippled. He pushed off from the window and began pacing in front of her. His movements were so fluid and graceful that even if Erica hadn't known he was a shifter, she would have suspected it in that moment.

"Look, Erica," Leo began, taking a deep breath before moving to sit on the coffee table in front of her. He was sitting so close to her, his knees rested on either side of hers. Erica's heart began to race just that little bit faster. With Ben sitting so close to her on the couch, she felt as if she were completely surrounded by them. "Ben and I are Enforcers for our pack, and that means we have taken an oath to protect our people and enforce the laws of our Alpha. At his request, we have been investigating the rise in the number of Fae who have ventured into our lands. The increase in number is proportionate to the number of missing humans, and we don't think that's just a coincidence."

Erica gasped. "Do you think I had something to do with this? That I am somehow kidnapping humans for some nefarious reason?"

Leo grimaced slightly, and Erica felt her heart drop to her stomach. "Well, despite the fact that I am going to completely contradict what I said earlier, no, I don't. I … hell, *we* don't think you would do that, or be capable of it."

Erica frowned. "That makes no sense. How can you accuse me of being here on a fact-finding mission for that fucking Alefric one minute, then turn around and tell me you don't think I'm capable of kidnapping and hurting humans the next?" She reached forward and placed the glass gently back on the table. When she went to pull her hand back, Leo caught it in his. A sizzle of awareness tinged with the electricity of attraction shot up her arm from her hand, making her gasp.

When she looked up to meet his gaze, she shivered at the heat in his eyes.

"I'm sorry. I went into Enforcer mode back there, despite what my heart and gut were telling me."

"What were they telling you?"

"That the Fates would never have given us a mate who would be capable of that."

Erica's jaw dropped as she replayed his words over in her head. Surely, she had misheard him?

"Erica." Ben spoke from her left, and she turned

her head to look in his direction. He smiled at her as he lifted a hand to gently lift her jaw and close her mouth. He then reached forward and gripped her left hand in his. The sensation was exactly the same as when Leo took her hand, and Erica drew in a deep breath at what that meant. "Do you know about wolf shifters and their mates?"

Erica nodded. She did know. Wolf shifters were often mated in triads, two male wolf shifters destined to be mated in truth to one female. That female would be the one to complete their bond, and the wolves would want no other than their fated mate. These two stunningly hot wolf shifters, with bodies, which despite being covered in clothing, Erica could tell would have a woman weeping for joy and pleasure just by looking at them—*they* were telling her that she was their fated mate.

"That's good. It makes it a little easier for you to know about our kind and what it would mean to be mated to us. But there is another thing that we need to share with you." Ben looked to his brother for a moment, and then returned his gaze to her. "When we were younger, a Fae woman came to Vancouver and befriended our pack. Although she never shared a whole hell of a lot with us about the Fae, claiming that it was not her place, she had the gift of foresight, and she told us a little about our mate."

"She told us that she would be unique among her people," Leo said, picking up where Ben left off. Erica turned to watch him as he spoke. "She mentioned that our mate would be hunted by her own kind. That she would possess an ability that would be coveted by many, and that we would need to keep her safe."

Erica sat back against the couch as her mind whirled with what she was being told. She was in no doubt that these two men were her Fated Ones, despite the fact it was rare for Fae to be mated outside of their own kind. Her head told her that it made sense, and what they were telling her resonated with what had been foretold about her own future many years ago. Her heart, already softening toward the two men, declared these two had the potential to fill the void that had existed within her heart since the day she lost her family.

And her body? Well, all the important girl parts were sizzling with the need to let them have her in any way they wanted. Now. Repeatedly.

"Well, I guess that's that then," Erica spoke softly, the importance of the moment not lost on her. "You are my Fated Ones, and I am your mate." She looked between her two men and smiled at the look of joy that spread across their handsome faces. "If Corrine gave you that much detail about me, then I guess she knew you were destined for me from the very beginning."

As soon as Ben and Leo began speaking of a Fae woman with the gift of foresight, defecting from the False King, she knew the woman had to be Corinne.

"You know Corrine?" Leo asked, surprise in his voice.

"Yeah, I do. In the Elven realm, she was my nanny and the confidante of my mother." Erica took a deep breath and made the decision in that moment to trust these men with whom she really was. "The Elf Queen."

Chapter Five

Leo stared at Erica in stunned silence. Their fated mate was a princess from beyond the Veil? How would they ever strive to be worthy of such a responsibility? Erica's circumstances would also put their pack in a very precarious place in this war. Harboring the rightful heir to the Elven throne could very possibly be something that not even their Alpha Gabe would be willing to risk. If that was the case, then they would have to leave their home, leave their pack, leave everything they had ever known to be with this woman. He could see the fear simmering behind the strength in her eyes as she sat and waited for their reaction. He reached up and brushed aside a lock of dark hair that kept falling over her forehead.

"Your parentage makes no difference to us, Erica. We will stand beside you no matter what. If the entire Fae army comes for you, they will still have to go through us to reach you," Leo concluded softly, leaning closer to Erica until his lips were a whisper away from hers.

He heard the low growl from his brother and knew that Ben had caught the seductive scent of her arousal in the air between them. She smelled like fresh summer strawberries, and Leo salivated to take a bite. He groaned when she closed the distance between them and wrapped her arms around his neck as she met his mouth with equal enthusiasm. The way she moved against him had his cock hardening at a painful rate. Goddess, he needed to be inside of this woman.

Leo could feel Ben move closer. They all *needed* to be closer. With a plan to make that happen in mind, he finally pulled back from her lips. Looking directly into her eyes, Leo slowly slid his hands down her breasts, reveling in the way her eyes went unfocused and her breathing increased. His palms were barely brushing down her sides, wanting to make his way to her pert but luscious ass that was just begging for his firm touch, but when his fingers caught on the material of her t-shirt, crusted with dry blood, even his wolf took a step back. Leo shook his head, disgusted with himself. Here he was, mauling his newly found mate while she was still covered in her own blood. Already, he felt as if he was failing her.

"I'm so sorry, love. I got carried away," he said, ashamed that his own carnal needs had made him forget that their mate needed to be taken care of.

"I think we all got a little carried away," she acknowledged with a low laugh, which had his cock twitching all over again.

"Finally, I'm officially more responsible than you, brother," Ben stated as he leaned forward and planted a quick kiss on Erica's lips before he stood and picked her up, cradling her in his arms. "Let's get you cleaned up, little pixie. Then you need some rest and time to absorb all of this."

The sound of her laughter again was enough to alleviate most of his guilt as he followed them out of the living room and down the hall to the master bathroom. Yes, their mate would bathe and rest … and then they would get back to claiming her. He stopped in the main bathroom to grab the first aid kit just in case they needed it, and when Leo turned the corner to see Erica standing there in nothing but her bra and panties, he almost walked into the door jamb. Even with the delicate pieces of lace being soaked in her blood, it wasn't enough to stop his desire for her. He couldn't keep the low growl to himself as he watched Ben's fingers check her now newly healed wounds.

"Like what you see, wolf?" she purred in a seductive low drawl. It seemed their little pixie had some exhibitionist in her because there was no doubt she liked having Leo's eyes on her while Ben's hands roamed. She licked her lips slowly, and then without breaking eye contact with Leo, she placed her hands over Ben's, and slowly drew them up to cup her breasts. Ben's groan was in sync with his own as her eyes closed like she was savoring his touch.

"Behave, you two!" Ben let out a frustrated growl as he gently pulled his hands away. "You've barely healed, pixie, and I'm trying to be the mature one here, but you're making it hard. You need to bathe and rest."

The little minx just smiled and looked pointedly down first at Ben's crotch and then at Leo's. There was no missing the erections they both had, and she seemed satisfied with their reaction, maybe even a little smug.

"Yes, I can see that they're *very hard* … and quite impressive, I might add." Erica's voice was pure desire as she took a step back from Ben and slowly removed her bra and panties. "Are you two coming?" she added with a wink before she turned and sauntered over to the large shower.

Leo almost had to laugh. He didn't think either Ben or himself had ever gotten undressed so fast before in their entire lives. Erica turned on the water and stepped inside. Leo had been so distracted by her shapely ass that he hadn't noticed his brother holding him back from following her at first.

"Remember, Leo, she's still hurt, so no sex," Ben warned low enough that Erica wouldn't hear it over the water.

"We'll just take care of her, and then put her to

bed," Leo agreed. They both then followed their seductress into the already steamed up shower.

Erica stood there looking every bit a goddess as the water poured over her. Her lithe body looked supple and strong, her breasts just more than a handful. *The perfect size*, Leo thought, and his mouth watered at the notion of sucking on her ripe berries. When he looked up and his eyes collided with her turquoise gaze, he forgot how to breathe. There would never be a more beautiful creature on this earth than their mate at this moment.

"I've never been this close to a wolf before," she whispered as her eyes roamed all over the two of them with obvious hunger. "I want to touch you both."

Ben growled low and deep in the back of his throat when Erica's hands began to trail slowly down his stomach. Then he took her hands in his own, raised them above her head, and pushed her back against the stone wall.

Now this was a game that Leo knew well. Their wolves were a naturally dominant part of their personality, and he enjoyed letting his wolf off the leash a little in the bedroom when it came to sex. He stepped up beside his brother and palmed Erica's breasts in a slow caress that had her moaning and pushing them further into his hands.

"You need rest, but first let us help you relax, little mate." Leo dropped to his knees in the water and ran his hands down her long legs, then pulled one up and placed it on his shoulder. He stared in awe at the beauty of her opened up before him. Leo didn't look up, but by the noises Ben and Erica were making, he knew that his brother was taking her mouth thoroughly. He leaned in at the apex of her thighs and scented her.

Goddess, fresh berries and cream. If she tasted a fraction as good as she smelled, he knew that he'd constantly be fighting his brother for a spot between her thighs. At the first long lick of his tongue along her wet slit, her hips bucked up and he had to grip her ass tight to keep her under control.

He was relentless in his pursuit of her pleasure, sucking and licking at her. When he finally slid two fingers into her molten core, she cried out and Leo felt her pussy spasm around his digits. He continued to draw one more time hard on her clit, and she came for him again bucking like a wildcat in their arms. The sight of her coming apart was enough to make Leo's cock ache for release, but since he knew that they wouldn't be taking her tonight, he let it sweep through him as he stroked himself and came seconds after her.

All three of them were breathing hard as Leo got back to his feet. Erica continued to sleepily kiss Ben, but he could see she was down for the count. It had been a very long night.

They finished bathing her quickly, washing the blood off of her. When they were done, Leo wrapped her in a towel and picked her up to carry her to the large bed in the middle of the room. As he settled her between the sheets and tucked her close to him, he felt his brother get in on the other side. A small sigh of contentment came from their mate as she snuggled into both of them. Leo knew at that moment that he'd never felt as happy as he did right then, and he'd do anything to keep this feeling.

Chapter Six

Ben awoke, not for the first time, in the middle of the night. Erica's delectable ass was once again pressed snugly against his crotch, and both his wolf and his iron stiff cock were twitching to finally claim their mate. He buried his nose in her dark, soft hair and inhaled her sweet scent, which did nothing to alleviate his current predicament.

He thought back to her bloodied body and the panic that had gripped him when he realized that they could lose her before even getting to know her. Even worse, that she could still be taken from them with the threat hanging over her. Fortunately and unfortunately, the dark thoughts doused some of his desire. Worry and anger took their place. Ben had known Erica less than twenty-four hours and already he knew that he would die before he'd let anything happen to her.

"We *will* protect her," he heard Leo whisper. Ben lifted his head to find Leo flat on his back with his arm thrown over his face.

"Fuck yeah!" Ben fiercely whispered back. And then Erica pushed back against his crotch, causing an involuntary moan to escape him. "Shut the fuck up," he threw at Leo, who laughed at his torture

"Hey, I share your pain, brother," Leo said, still chuckling. "Our little pixie here was pressed up against my cock earlier."

Just then, Erica moaned. Ben smiled, thinking perhaps she may be having a naughty dream about him and his brother until her moans turned into whimpers. A strangled sob escaped her, and she began to struggle against him. Ben just held her tighter—afraid that she would hurt herself—cooing softly in her ear, "You're safe, sweetheart. Shhh."

"We've got you," Leo added.

Their reassurances did nothing to comfort her it seemed, as she continued to moan and thrash in Ben's arms. Leo had to help restrain her as well.

"I'll kill you. I'll kill you," she called out like a mantra. A white glow began to emanate from her body, causing a painful jolt to run through Ben's arms, but he held her steady and gritted his teeth through the pain. He looked over to find Leo in the same predicament. He wondered how many Fae scum he would have to turn to ash before he finally considered his pixie avenged.

Erica let out a piercing scream before she finally jerked awake. Ben and Leo still held on tightly to her.

"What? Where am I?" A few more minutes passed before Erica finally realized where she was. "Oh, gods! I am so sorry," she said, withdrawing the pain inducing glow. "I can't believe I did that to you."

"You did what you had to do," Ben replied, his voice still raspy and his body still shivering from her burst of energy. He'd have to file away this other ability of hers for later. *Interesting,* he thought. He had never recalled a Fae having the power to hurt and weaken before, but then again, he never imagined he'd come across a self-healing one either. "What did they do to you, Erica?"

"Please," she pleaded. "Don't make me talk about it now. I … can't. I need … I need…"

"Tell us," Ben asked softly, still hugging her from behind. "Tell us what you need and you can have it."

Erica turned her head to look at him and then turned to look at Leo. "You. I need the both of you. I need my mates."

Ben's heart broke at the sound of the desperation in her voice. He still worried that perhaps because of her earlier injuries, making love to her now would be too soon, but he could not deny her anything. And the thought of not claiming his mate right now escalated almost to the point of being painful for both him and his wolf.

He'd be gentle, he thought reassuringly.

He'd definitely at least try to be gentle, he promised himself.

Calm the fuck down, he mentally reprimanded his wolf, who frantically chuffed like a dog in heat.

Then Leo took Erica's mouth in a passionate kiss, and Ben began to slowly trail kisses from the back of her neck all the way down her spine. He disentangled himself from her beautiful body and sat up on his haunches to admire her naked form. The bed sheets had been thrown off earlier during her struggles. Leo shifted Erica onto her back and trailed his own kisses on her neck, then her collarbone, before his mouth latched on to one of her soft, rose-colored nipples. Erica threw her head back and let out a loud moan.

"Is he making you feel good, baby?"

Her response was unintelligible but Ben was certain she meant it in the affirmative. Then her legs parted in invitation for him to finally devour what Leo had had the pleasure of tasting earlier. He reached forward, spreading her thighs wider and bent his head to inhale her sweet and earthy scent.

Euphoria.

He licked a path across her slit and discovered that her taste was even more delicious than her scent, all sweetness with a hint of spice. He fervently devoured her. And to add even more pleasure to his current state, Erica must have realized that she was in prime position to stroke his rock hard cock. She started slowly, fisting up and down his shaft, adding a twist every now and then after she must have felt him shiver the first time she did it. She dutifully discovered how to play him as he ate her like a man who had never tasted something more delicious.

"Fuck!" Ben roared against her pussy. She had nearly unhinged him when her grip became tighter and her travels began to include brushing the underside of his mushroomed head. Ben lifted his head to look down at what Erica was doing to him, but he did not leave her bereft of his touch. He inserted two fingers into her soaked opening and with his thumb now circling her clit, began to pump them in and out of her. Her hips bucked wildly when he found that sweet spot against her vaginal wall. When her inner muscles tightened around his fingers, he knew she was about to come all over them. His own orgasm rose to the surface.

"Come for me, Erica," he commanded just before he bent his head back down and sucked her clit into his mouth. He placed his forearm across her thighs, holding her in place as she rode out her orgasm, moaning, calling out his name. She was still screaming it as he found his release. Erica held onto his cock, letting him spill across her stomach as if by instinct she knew that his mark of territory would please his wolf. She was made for them.

Leo looked honored as well by Erica's action and moved aside to give her and Ben a moment. Ben's lips quirked at Erica's sly smile. Their little minx knew exactly what she was doing. He leaned forward and kissed her. His tongue danced with hers in languid strokes, sparking a brand new fire inside of him.

He hadn't even realized that Leo had left the room until he returned with a washcloth for Erica. Ben took it from Leo's outstretched hand and wiped Erica's belly clean, before wiping his now hardening cock. He couldn't wait to be inside her, to feel the walls of her pussy tighten around his shaft, but he knew that his brother was just as desperate. He also knew that as the older brother, Leo should claim their mate first. Regardless, they would all be firmly mated before morning.

Chapter Seven

"Damn," Leo began, "that was the hottest thing I have ever seen."

Erica smiled at the need-ravaged sound of Leo's voice behind her. When she managed to pry her eyes open, she turned in Ben's arms to smile at Leo over her shoulder.

"Mmmm, it felt pretty damn hot, too," she murmured in a voice made raspy by screaming Ben's name at the top of her lungs. "I have never come so hard and I should be absolutely satisfied, but I'm not." Rolling onto her back, she held her hand out toward Leo, spreading her legs slowly to show him her wet, glistening, and very needy pussy in all its glory. From the spark of desire that immediately flared in his eyes, Erica knew Leo was riding the same knife's edge to remain in control.

Erica slid both hands down her torso and reached between her legs. Wanting to see her mate's control shatter, she decided to tug on her wolf's tail. Using the fingers of her right hand, she stimulated her own clit and slid the index and middle fingers of her left hand deep inside her pussy. She moaned out loud at the double stimulation but made sure to maintain eye contact with her mate. Leo's eyes glittered, his wolf very much near the surface. "Leo, I need you, baby. Come fuck me, please?" Erica removed her fingers from her pussy and raised them toward her mouth.

They never reached her intended target. Leo moved lightning fast to lie over the top of her, his hips nestled in the natural cradle of her own, and gripped her wrist with his hand.

"Oh, hell no, my beautiful little pixie." Leo's wolf

was so close, his canines already dropping in readiness to claim her, his voice, slightly distorted. "It took every ounce of strength I possess to stand still and enjoy that little show you just put on. And just so you know, one of these days we are going to insist that you take that little show right through to the final curtain."

Erica's pussy leaked at the thought of masturbating in front of her men. She never knew she had such a strong exhibitionist streak within her.

"But for now," Leo went on, "I think I deserve a little treat for having the willpower of a fucking saint."

Erica gasped as Leo tugged her hand to his mouth and sucked into his mouth the fingers still glistening wet with the proof of her desire. Her gasp turned into a deep moan at the feel of his tongue swirling between and around her fingers and the strong suction he applied to ensure he got every last drop. Erica began to pant as her arousal spiraled quickly into her "imminent spontaneous combustion zone", and her pussy leaked her arousal.

"Fuck, I can smell her sweet pussy with every damn breath I take," Ben spoke from where he lay on the bed beside them, his gaze steady on her. "You'd better fuck her now, brother, or I'm gonna have to take over. Our mate needs some loving!"

Leo's lips turned up in a smile that screamed wicked intent, and Erica shivered at what that could mean for her. "You could try and get me to move, little brother, but unless you're packing some C-4 that just ain't gonna happen." He rolled his hips forward, pressing the hot, hard tip of his cock against the swollen lips of her pussy. "Now, little pixie, I, too, can tell that you are feeling more than just a little needy, and it is now my mission in life to make sure you get everything—" he pushed his hips forward, and Erica felt the head of his cock slide just inside her, "you—" another roll buried him even further within her and she moaned arching her back at the feeling, "need!" With that final word, he slammed to the hilt within her.

So sensitive from her orgasm just minutes before, she screamed at the sensation of being completely taken. Leo paused for a moment, and Erica relaxed her body as sparks of pleasure began to burst within her, and she rolled her hips in silent entreaty for him to move. True to his word to give her what she needed, he began to shuttle his hips, driving in and out of her in a steady rhythm.

Erica moaned as he added a swift swivel of his hips on the downward thrust, which ground his body against her engorged clit. "Oh gods!" She groaned as her orgasm began to build within her so fast and so high she was almost frightened by its intensity.

Leo lifted up onto his arms and began to pound into her. Erica had always considered herself to be an active participant in all things sexual, so she lifted her feet and placed them on the mattress, giving her the leverage to lift her hips to meet his thrusts.

Leo's eyes slammed shut, and he threw his head back with a growl. "Fuck, Erica! Yeah, baby, that's it. Take what you need from your mate. Fuck me, pixie!"

Erica lost herself to the feel of her mate. She floated within a sea of sensation as she felt every muscle in her body begin to tense when the tsunami that was her orgasm threatened to crash over her. She felt her canines extend and knew that the moment was almost upon her. For the Fae, finding their Fated One triggered a visceral need to mark them with a claiming bite that announced to the world that they were spoken for, and also, much like a wolf, though significantly smaller, their canines extended.

Erica felt the first quiver of ecstasy within that

told her she was moments from shattering. With her last thread of conscious thought, she pulled Leo down to her and bit deep into the fleshy part of his shoulder.

"Erica!" Leo roared as the exotic flavor of him exploded across her tongue, and her body shuddered with rapture as her orgasm rolled through her. She moaned as Leo started pounding within her harder and faster than he had before, and she swept her tongue across the wound she left behind, pouring some of her power into it to heal the small punctures.

Releasing him, she pulled back and drew in a huge gulp of air, which erupted in a scream when she felt Leo shudder above her. A white-hot pain struck the side of her neck. The pain morphed quickly into pleasure, and an orgasm larger and more intense than the one she was still enjoying the aftershocks of, hit with the force of a freight train.

"Leo!" she screamed his name, a thread of fear in her tone as she was thrown through a maelstrom of pleasure the likes of which she had never known existed. She and Leo shuddered together as their shared release gently rocked to a halt within them. Erica fought to control her rapidly beating heart that seemed to be on the verge of exploding, and Leo slumped over her with a groan, just stopping himself from collapsing completely upon her.

"Holy shit," Leo groaned beside her ear and Erica gasped a breathy laugh.

Yeah, that about summed it up.

She felt the mattress shift beside her and turned to look at Ben where he lay beside them. He held his engorged cock with his hand, tight at the base. "Fucking hell, pixie. The sight of you coming apart like that, and claiming my brother just moments before he claimed you almost had me coming like an untried pup."

Erica grinned, still panting a little, and though her heart rate began to return to normal, seeing Ben lying there deliciously stroking his cock, had her pussy tightening in need again.

"Shit," Leo muttered then groaned as he pushed up on his arms, gently withdrawing his semi hard cock. "I felt that. Ben, our mate is in need of some more loving, and it is most definitely your turn." Leo pressed a sweet kiss to her lips before collapsing with a groan beside her. "Fuck me, do you think it is going to be that damn explosive between us every time we fuck our mate?"

Erica giggled as she turned toward Ben, and began to crawl in his direction. "I have no idea, but as of right now? I am all about finding out!"

Chapter Eight

"Over you go, baby." As soon as Erica had reached Ben, he flipped her over on her belly, pulling a surprised squeak from her in the process. He then pulled her up to her knees and trailed one of his hands down her back, while the other held firmly to her hip. "Gods, I love this ass." His hand stopped on her backside and massaged it in slow circles. He pulled another surprised squeak from her when he bent forward and licked all the way from her seam to her puckered hole.

"I'm gonna have this ass soon, too," he added. When he licked her there again, she moaned and pushed her ass backward for more.

"I think she likes that idea, little brother," Leo said from his reclined position. "The two of us fucking her together."

"Yes. Yes!" Erica panted. "Please, do it now."

"You have no idea how happy that makes me to hear." Ben licked her again, eliciting another moan— louder and more drawn out than the one before. He couldn't wait for the three of them to experience that moment of truly being one, but now was not the time. "We will need to prepare you first, Erica. You may be self-healing and all, but I don't want you to have to. The first time I take you there, I want it to feel so fucking good for you that you won't be able to help but beg for more."

"Oh—"

Without warning, and in one long stroke, Ben plunged into her tight, wet pussy. He pushed in all the way to the hilt while holding on tightly to her hips. He held her there, savoring the moment of being fully seated inside of her. Warmth surrounded him. His body tingled from head to toe. And then he had no choice but to move.

His strokes remained long and hard, and each time he pulled in, he'd hold himself there for a beat before pulling almost all the way out again. His hands wandered down her back to her ass and back up again, wanting to touch and memorize the feel of every part of her. He attuned himself to the sound of her heart beating and pleasurable cries, his own sounds and heartbeat becoming in sync with hers.

When he lowered himself so that his front touched her back, he picked up the pace and his thrusts became faster and harder. This time, as he balanced himself on one hand, his other hand memorized the curves of her front. He played with her breasts, massaging them, plucking at her nipples, drew slow circles around her stomach, and worked his way down even lower to her mound and slid his fingers through her wet flesh.

His orgasm was going to be explosive. He felt it impending upon them both. Erica whimpered and mewled and then finally begged him to make her come. Ben knew that he would never deny her anything. His fingers focused solely on her clit as he fiercely drove his cock into her from behind. When he licked the shell of her ear, Erica screamed. Within moments, Ben was coming as well, Erica still spasming, her velvet walls squeezing him hard.

But he wasn't done with her yet. He pulled out, flipped her over so that she was flat on her back, and shoved back into her. Meanwhile, his canines elongated when his lips found her neck, and he sank them into her flesh, tasting and swallowing down the copper ambrosia inside. He felt a pleasurable sting on the side of his neck. Her taste combined with the feeling of his blood and essence being pulled into Erica's mouth, was more intense than anything he had ever felt before. He found himself, unbelievably, hard and coming again, almost violently inside of her, Erica's second climax matching his. They both shuddered and held on to each other, neither ready to let go yet. He licked the mark he'd inflicted on her neck, effectually sealing it, and Erica followed suit with the mark she had given him.

Ben lifted himself on his forearms to gaze at Erica. Her eyes were half-lidded and sleepy as she looked up at him with awe and possibly … love? He couldn't help but smile. He was pretty much there himself already. The connection among the three of them was so strong now that he thought about it. He had felt its pull leading them into that alleyway earlier today.

Ben rolled off of her and lay on his side facing her, Leo mirroring the move. They each held one of Erica's hands in theirs, gazing down at the woman who was their destiny, before locking eyes with each other. Without speaking, Ben knew that he and Leo were on the same page. Tomorrow they would plot. The Fae King was dead, whether he knew it or not, and so were all the Fae fuckers who ever harmed their mate or aided the ones who did.

"What happens now?" Erica asked softly.

Ben smiled down at her and kissed her forehead. "Now we get some sleep."

Chapter Nine

Leo awoke the next morning feeling more rested than he could ever remember, rested and happy. As he turned his head to look at his mate and his brother both still fast asleep in the bed next to him, he had to touch his chest at the feeling of joy that bubbled up, knowing Erica was safe and theirs to keep. He'd never paid much attention to the other mated males in their pack before when they'd talked about the feeling of completeness they experienced after claiming their mate, but that's exactly what it was. Erica had come into their lives and filled a hole in his soul that he hadn't even noticed existed. It seemed ridiculous to compare the feelings and emotions he'd felt in the past for other females. It was like comparing a tiny flickering flame to the heat and brilliance of the sun. The memory of every other woman had been scorched from his brain the first time he'd looked into her beautiful eyes.

Leo was literally sitting there watching her sleep like a lovesick teenager. He quickly got out of bed before he found himself unable to leave. Someone had to make breakfast for their mate, after all, and he knew his brother was *not* a morning person. He grabbed his cell phone off the dresser as he pulled on a pair of sweats and made his way into the kitchen. He needed to call Gabe and update him on what had happened last night. Leo had to admit that he was a bit nervous about telling Gabe everything. Their mating would no doubt impact a lot of wolves, and as much as he loved his life here, he would leave with Erica and Ben if Gabe thought it was too large a risk to keep her here.

He started the potatoes and put the bacon in the oven to cook before he called his Alpha. Erica's needs came first. From now on, she would always come first. *Especially in the bedroom,* he thought to himself with a chuckle, figuring that's how his cheeky brother would have responded to that particular statement if he'd said it out loud.

"Leo, what the hell happened last night?" Gabe barked out as soon as he answered the call. "I was starting to get worried when you didn't report in, but it didn't feel like you were in danger." Gabe was always intuitive like that when it came to the members of his pack.

"Sorry, Gabe, we picked up a scent at the Viper Lounge while on patrol last night and ended up in a fight with several Fae Royal Guards."

"Fuck. What the hell are Royal Guards doing in our city?" Gabe muttered, clearly concerned. "Another human was taken last night."

"Shit," Leo spat. Gabe assuaged his guilt by reassuring him that there was nothing he or Ben could have done. The human had been taken from a bar across town, the stench of Fae all over the scene.

Leo figured he might as well tell Gabe the rest. "There's more. They were hunting a female, Gabe ... our female. Ben and I found our mate last night."

"Congratulations, Leo, I know you've been waiting a long time. Is she all right? Am I right in assuming all of the Fae were taken care of?"

"They were, Alpha, and yes, she is fine. But there is one more detail that you need to know about our mate before we bring her to meet you today."

"Fuck, Leo, just spit it out already. I've never known you to beat around the bush like this."

Leo sighed and decided to just get it over with.

"Our mate is Fae, and she is the rightful heir to the throne. She escaped from Alefric's custody a few years ago, and that's what brought his guards here. They had finally picked up on her trail."

Leo met silence on the other end of the line, and he could almost hear the wheels turning in his Alpha's brain as he assessed all the angles and risks. Leo held his breath hoping that Gabe would offer her sanctuary within the pack, but this was a complication they simply couldn't have ever imagined.

Finally, his Alpha answered. "Bring her to my home. It will be safest for her here."

"Thank you, Alpha," was all Leo said before he hung up the phone.

Leo had just poured himself a cup of coffee when he felt the arousal of his mate through their bond. His cock became instantly hard, tenting out his sweatpants, and by the other emotions he was feeling, his brother and his mate were both now very much awake. He tried to ignore his own state of arousal as he started the eggs and toast. No doubt it was the smell of bacon that had woken his brother in the first place.

He was just placing the plate of eggs in the oven when he felt Erica's hands smooth over his back as she hugged him from behind.

"Morning, love, how did you sleep?" he asked her as he closed the oven and stood back up, wrapping his arms over hers.

"Very well, thank you. *Mmmm,* that smells good. I'm starving." Her sneaky little hands moved over his hot skin, down his abs, and slipped under the front of his sweatpants to curl her fingers around his still throbbing shaft.

"Fuck," he groaned out as she stroked him slowly up and down.

"Yes, we did," she replied, "and now we should

fuck again."

"Thank the gods you cooked, Leo. I'm starving!" Ben said as he barreled into the kitchen, completely ignoring that their mate had her hands currently down his pants.

When Erica's hand stopped moving and Leo felt her start to giggle behind him at Ben's oblivious beeline to the food, he couldn't help but join her, and they both burst out laughing. He turned in her arms and kissed her good morning.

"Rain check, baby. Let's get you fed." Leo pushed Erica toward a chair at the breakfast bar and handed her a steaming cup of coffee. "Once we're done eating, we'll head out to Gabe's place."

Ben's fork stopped directly in front of his mouth at Leo's words. "You called the Alpha?"

"I did."

"You told him everything?" Ben placed his fork back on the plate. "And he told us to bring Erica out to his place?"

Leo just nodded at his brother, and he could see the relief in his brother's eyes that their Alpha would extend the pack's protection to their mate.

****

"It's very beautiful here," Erica remarked as they crossed the Lions Gate Bridge and left the city behind them.

Vancouver was a beautiful place, surrounded by the mountains and the ocean. Anyone would be remiss to find a spot where nature could not be visible in all of her glory, the perfect place for shifters to blend in with their surroundings and raise their families. At least, it was perfect until the Fae had begun to show themselves more and more.

They got off the highway and drove up the

mountain, and the properties got larger and larger, the houses more extravagant, until finally they arrived at the gravel driveway that led up to Gabe's house.

"Here we are," Leo said as they parked. Then all three of them got out of the truck.

The front door opened, and their Alpha walked out with a dainty, strawberry blonde female by his side. Her big gray eyes stared directly at Erica. Leo heard his mate's sharp inhale as they were greeted.

"Eyrica, child? Is that you?" Corrine's words were spoken barely above a whisper, the shock of seeing Erica written clear across her face. The elder Fae smiled at her, flashing her dimples. She then rushed forward toward Erica, pulling her into a tight embrace.

Chapter Ten

"Quenya," Erica whispered the Elven word for "nanny" in awe, before she wrapped her arms around the slight woman, then lowered her head to Corrine's shoulder and sobbed. As she inhaled, she drew the scent of clementines and vanilla into her lungs, and the familiarity of it made her cry even harder as she was suddenly flooded with memories.

Her childhood had been filled with love, laughter, and joy from times where Corrine and Erica's parents spent afternoons doing nothing but play with her, to evenings spent with them reading her stories, each of them taking a role and acting it out for her. Her father would often choose a romantic story, and when the hero kissed the heroine, he'd capitalize on the opportunity to dip her mother over his arm and kiss her, making Erica and Corrine giggle. But it was the final memory that remained most vivid for her.

The day she'd lost both her parents.

They were having dinner in the main hall when the doors burst open. Before he could even get up from the table, her father was killed with an arrow to the heart, pinning him to the chair. Three men, who now formed the senior ranks of Alefric's guard, stormed the room. One of them grabbed her mother and dragged her from her chair. Corrine leapt to her feet to try to intervene but was knocked to the ground. The third moved to stand behind Erica's chair, resting a hand heavily on her shoulder.

Erica was struck with grief as she watched the light drain from her father's eyes, but it was quickly replaced by anger when she watched one of the guards, his arm wrapped around her mother's neck, lift a knife with a curved blade, and hold it against the soft skin of her throat.

"Your time is up, Your Highness, *" the man spat the final two words. It was clear he felt nothing for her mother but contempt. "Alefric demands your answer. Now!"*

Tears slid down Raelyn's cheeks as she stared at her husband, no doubt looking for any signs of life. "You've killed him, my Haydrian," she cried.

The guard closest to her father's body barked a laugh. "Yes, we did. You were warned about what would happen if you weren't willing to do what Alefric wanted. Did you think he was just going to let it go?"

Erica watched as her mother seemed to stand taller, the tears ceasing altogether and her face filling with disgust. "No, I never thought that Alefric would let it go. But I believed he had the intelligence to know that what he was asking for would never be willingly given. The right to rule this realm is through bloodlines. Alefric's bloodline is evil and toxic and will never be worthy of our throne."

"That's why he wanted you to marry him, you stupid bitch," the man behind her snarled. "All you had to do was agree to marry a male with the strength to make the Fae a force to be reckoned with, the way we all know we should be! You and that spineless bastard you married wanted alliances and treaties with animals. Shifters should have only one role in life and that is to serve the Fae."

"Serve the Fae?" her mother said incredulously. "Why would they agree to that? Shifters are a strong, loyal, and a proud race. Whatever gives you the idea that they would simply fall into lives of servitude to anyone, let alone a race they know very little about?"

"Because that is as it should be!"

Erica turned toward the voice that echoed through the broken doorway. She gulped at the look on the face of the Fae male who walked through the door. He wore the blazer of a high ranked member of her parents' military. His long black hair fell down his back, braided at his temples. His dark green eyes and his face were filled with rage. "The Fae should be the most revered and feared race on either side of the Veil, and yet you want to disgrace our heritage and live alongside these animals in harmony? You are a fool, Raelyn! We will no longer sit idly by and allow you to disgrace us as you have been.

"Now, I am tired of waiting for you to do the right thing, so as you can see, we are taking matters into our own hands. I am taking my rightful place as the King of this realm, and you can either take your place at my side or die by his." Alefric sneered as he motioned to her beloved husband's now still body. "The choice is simple."

Erica's heart began to pound when her mother turned to look at her, her eyes filled with pain and grief, but also begging her for forgiveness. She knew in that moment that her mother had already made her decision. If she hadn't known her mother as well as she did, Erica might have missed the small throwing knife that slipped from her mother's sleeve and into her hand.

"Over a future with you?" Raelyn sneered as she turned to glare at Alefric. "I most certainly choose death. And it is my will that I take you with me, you murdering bastard!" And with a scream of defiance, her mother let the knife fly. From where Erica sat still pinned to her chair, the trajectory of the knife looked true, but there was a reason Alefric had risen so high and so quickly within their army's ranks. He turned at the very last moment to take the knife in his shoulder.

Elena Kincaid, Maia Dylan, and Sarah Marsh

*Alefric groaned and hunched forward, the knife
still embedded in his flesh. "Kill that bitch," he roared,
and then things moved in what seemed to be slow motion
for Erica. Corrine screamed and launched herself from
the floor and in her mother's direction. The guard behind
her mother gripped her hair, arching her neck and began
to draw the blade with deadly accuracy across Raelyn's
throat. The arc of blood was the last thing Erica
remembered of that day, before she fell into
unconsciousness, the grief of watching both her parents
killed in front of her too much to bear for a child so
young. The soundtrack playing in the background was
her own screams of horror.*

"Shh, child," Corrine murmured gently, bringing
Erica out of her memories and back into the present.
Somehow she had been led further into the house and
now sat on a couch, still held tightly in Corrine's arms.
"You're going to make yourself ill, and from the looks of
concern and anger on the faces of your young mates here,
I think that might just throw them over the edge and into
insanity."

With a small hiccup-laugh, Erica raised her head
to look for her mates. Ben sat beside her, gently stroking
his hand down her back, and Leo knelt on the floor in
front of her. Corrine was right. Both of them looked
anxious and ready to kill at the same time. "It is so good
to see you, *Quenya*. For the longest time, I thought you
were dead. When Leo and Ben spoke of a Fae woman
with a seer's gift yesterday, I just knew they were
speaking about you. I felt it in my very soul."

Corrine made a *tsk* sound and reached up to
cradle Erica's face in her hands. "You should have
known better than to doubt me, child. I am a survivor,
just like you."

Erica nodded and smiled. Corrine had been more than just her nanny. She had also been her mother's most trusted advisor. The gods would share visions with her of what would or could happen in the future. If her visions were meant to be taken as a warning rather than prediction, then they were sometimes given time to change the path to ensure a different outcome.

"After I was unable to save your mother, Alefric had me taken to the dungeons. He knew of my foresight ability and wanted me to advise him. I stayed for a while, simply feeding him the information he wanted to know. I knew that with Raelyn dead, his attentions would turn toward you." A low continuous growling filled the room. "And well may you growl, wolf mates to my princess. There are a large number within the Fae that look to him as their leader, but a growing faction awaits the true bloodline of their Fae royalty to return. The only chance he has of uniting the two is to take our Erica as his mate. I told him that Erica must not be mated until after her twenty-first birthday."

And wasn't that just a delightful thought. Erica shuddered at the thought of being mated to the narcissistic asshole and barked a humorless laugh. "Well, that explains why he came to me the day after my birthday."

"He what?" Leo asked his voice deadly.

"He tried to get me to *cooperate*. Gave me twenty-four hours to think things over."

"He dies, hard," Ben growled, his wolf clear in his voice.

Corrine grinned, and Erica knew she approved of both of her wolves. "Now that I would love to see, but I have yet to be shown the death that awaits him."

"Have you seen what lies ahead for us?" Ben asked.

Corrine's smile slipped away and a shadow formed in her eyes. "I have seen two possible outcomes for your future, and as with all battles between good and evil, there is a happy ending and one that is not so happy."

Having forgotten that the Alpha still sat in the room, Erica startled slightly when Gabe sat forward in the seat he had taken across the room. "Corrine, you talk as if there is already a battle on the horizon, but you have never spoken of this before."

"You are already at war, Gabe, and it is one that you must win. Not just to guarantee the happiness of these three young lovers—" Corrine gestured between Erica and her mates, "but the survival of your own pack. I have never spoken of this as I had not been shown every piece of the puzzle that is unfolding before us, and there is much that still remains in the dark."

Gabe's face turned fierce. "What in the hell do you mean the survival of my pack? Who in the hell would be crazy enough to fuck with a pack as strong as ours?"

"Alefric is," Erica answered gently. "He is more than crazy enough to start that war, and he's also vain enough to believe that there would be no real threat to him once this war begins."

Corrine sighed and nodded. "That is very true, child, but, Gabe, there is more to this than what I see. Can you be assured that your pack is as strong as you think? I pray for all our sakes that it is, because if there is even one small opportunity for Alefric to infiltrate and sway the odds in his favor, he will find a way to do it."

The room fell silent as they each thought about what that could mean. Wanting to fill the silence, Erica asked, "What were the outcomes you saw for us,

Quenya?"

Corrine turned to look at her, and Erica's heart pounded at the sadness in her eyes. "There will come a moment, where you will be faced with your greatest challenge. Alefric will stand before you, and a battle will ensue. If you are unable to kill him, then you will lose your opportunity at happiness. If—"

"I don't think," Ben interrupted, "that either Leo or I will have any qualms about ripping that fucker's throat out. Ending him will be a fucking pleasure."

"That may be true, young wolf, and I do hope that you get that opportunity, but the job of ending that Fae's life may fall to your mate. Destiny can be a fickle mistress in derailing the best-laid plans."

Erica nodded. She didn't have the foresight Corrine had, but she had always felt that there would be a showdown of sorts between her and Alefric. In fact, she was looking forward to it. She owed him far worse for the death of her parents.

Before Leo and Ben could voice the objections Erica read on both their faces, another man walked into the room. He was tall and built like he'd been born in a gym. His dark hair was cropped short to his head, and a tribal tattoo of some sort wrapped around his forearm. "Alpha, there is a Fae emissary here with a message for you."

Again the room fell into silence. Now that was unexpected.

"What is the message, Donovan?" Gabe snarled.

The shifter shrugged, folding his arms across his chest. "I have no clue, Alpha. I explained to him that I was your Beta and could bring the message to you, but he was adamant that the message was for your ears only."

Erica watched as a feral grin bloomed on the Alpha's face. "Well then, it would be very rude of me not to give that message my *complete* attention." Gabe and his Beta then strode out of the room.

"What if our pixie is successful?" Ben asked, placing a hand high on her thigh. "I mean, I would much prefer it is me or Leo that gets to tangle with this fucker, but if it has to be Erica, then I have faith she will divest him of his head quickly and efficiently."

Erica smiled gently and placed her own hand on top of his. "You have that much faith in me?"

Leo snorted, leaning in to place his hands on both her knees. "Honey, we both do. You forget, we saw the way you swung that deadly looking curved blade of yours. If there is a fight between the two of you and it is fair, then we have no doubt that you will send him to the hell he deserves. But make no mistake … I have no intention of allowing this to be a fair fight."

Erica felt the final dark spot in her heart fill with the light of the love for both these men and knew they owned her completely.

"Then your happily ever after will be filled with the love and laughter you all deserve," Corrine answered, filling Erica with hope.

The sound of snarling, growling, and screaming came from the front of the house, and all four of them leaped to their feet. Leo and Ben moved to stand in a protective position in front of her and Corrine. Just as Erica was about to suggest they go and see what the ruckus was, the door Gabe and Donovan had exited through opened, and Gabe strode back into the room. Naked.

Leo growled low, moved to a sideboard, opened a drawer, and threw his Alpha a pair of running shorts. "What the hell was all that about?"

Gabe pulled on the shorts, his eyes still flashing

with signs of his wolf. "It would seem that this Alefric prick has decided he wants your Fae back. He has given us forty-eight hours to return the princess, or we go to war, and the Fae will not stop until every single one of my pack is dead … so they said."

Leo stepped closer to her. Erica couldn't help but wonder if being mated to Leo and Ben would ultimately drive a wedge between her mates and their Alpha. "And what was your answer?"

Gabe's scowl morphed into a bloodthirsty grin. "I ripped off the Fae prick's right arm and left him for Donovan to chew on for a bit. No one threatens me and mine, not if they expect to live. And if he sends his messenger into the den of an Alpha like me, then he'd best be prepared for the consequences."

****

"The message has been received, my King."

Alefric turned from his position at the window to see Kheelan standing in the doorway.

"Where is the Fae who delivered the message? Bring him to me. I want to know if there was any return message."

Kheelan made a strange face. "We found the messenger this morning near the clearing in the woods where we entered the human realm to deliver the original message to the Alpha. The wolves must have tracked his scent back to that location and left him there for us to find … well, what was left of him anyway." Kheelan elaborated that the messenger had gasped his last few breaths as they stumbled upon him, and then turned to ash before they could send him back through the portal.

Alefric grinned, beckoning Kheelan forward. "And that would be a message in and of itself, now wouldn't it? It would appear that the shifter Alpha thinks to take the challenge and go to war."

"I am glad this news pleases you, my lord," Kheelan replied as he moved toward his King, a look of pure lust upon his face as he dropped to his knees before Alefric, reaching for the buttons on his trousers. "But may I ask why it pleases you so?"

Alefric growled low as Kheelan gently drew his hard cock from his trousers and bent his head to take him immediately to the back of his throat. Alefric reached down, gripped Kheelan's hair in both hands and began to fuck his mouth with hard thrusts of his hips. "Because the battle is lost to him already, he just doesn't know it yet."

Chapter Eleven

"*Quenya?* What is it?" Erica asked with concern. Gabe had just left the room to make some phone calls—and possibly to put on some more clothes—when Corinne's eyes went unfocused as if she'd entered some trance. Ben had only heard her visions after she had already had them. He had never been present for them before. He did not, however, imagine her face to look as completely ashen as it did now. No wonder his pixie was concerned. Whatever Corinne was envisioning had him concerned as well, even more so when the knowledgeable Fae's hands began to tremble.

"Please, *Quenya,* please…" Erica took both Corinne's hands in hers while Leo sat behind her and rubbed circles on her back to try to soothe her. Leo looked just as concerned, however.

"Let the vision finish, sweetness," Ben said quietly as he sat on the floor beside Erica's legs. "She will tell us when it's over."

Erica nodded and continued to hold Corrine's hand until her eyes returned to normal. Corrine still looked overly pale, and when she smoothly removed her hands from Erica's hold, Ben noticed that they were still shaking.

"There is or will be a foe amongst friends," Corinne croaked. Her voice sounded as if she had just woken up and it was still rough with sleep.

"Who?" Leo barked from behind Erica.

"We'll kill that motherfucker now," Ben chimed in. "Problem solved."

Ben could feel a vein bulging by his right temple. As if they didn't have enough heavy shit to deal with already, a traitorous scumbag just had to be added to the mix.

"I can't see clearly who it will be just yet." Corinne's voice held an unmistakable quiver. There was more to her vision than what she was letting on, Ben thought. "Perhaps the traitor will decide against their actions and what I saw will not come to pass."

"What did you see exactly?" Leo asked. He scooped Erica up and placed her on his lap. Their poor little pixie had already been through so much. A traitor may end up tipping the scales in Alefric's favor if they couldn't get the situation under control quickly.

"My visions aren't always direct. I see symbols almost like in a deck of Tarot cards, and foreboding shadows. Sometimes I see the people concerned and their expressions tell me everything I need to know—"

"With all due respect, Corinne," Ben interrupted, "we would love to hear about the intricacies of your visions, but we are pressed for time." He felt bad almost immediately after uttering those words, but his priority now was stopping the threat to his woman and his pack. Furthermore, he was anxious to probe her for more information on whatever she saw that he was sure she was about to withhold.

"Patience is a virtue, young wolf," Corrine said, "but I will appease you for the sake of your poor nerves. I saw a dove flying through the air, carrying a message stained with blood and…"

"And?" Ben prompted.

Corrine took a deep breath. She seemed to turn something over in her head before she continued. "I saw the point of departure and destination. The dove flew from this house and went straight through the Veil."

Ben heard a sharp intake of breath from Erica. No doubt she was familiar with the symbolism of Corinne's visions.

"What else did you see, *Quenya?*"

His pixie missed nothing either, and when he locked eyes with Leo, he was positive that all three of them were on the same page.

"Nothing more," Corinne adamantly said. "I am sure the vision will become clearer when it is meant to. Perhaps I shall see the face of the betrayer before anything comes to pass." She then stood abruptly. "Excuse me a moment. These visions sometimes take a toll on me. I need some air."

"I'll come with you." Erica gave Leo a light squeeze before she disentangled herself from his arms and stood from his lap.

Holding up her hand, Corrine said, "No, child. I need a moment alone. Perhaps if I concentrate, I shall see more. Besides," she added when she was almost out of the room, "I think your men have a need to attend to you." Corinne winked and then left the room.

She failed at making light of the situation, and as much as he wanted to ravage his pixie right then and there, they needed to talk first.

And then we ravage her.

"Pipe down!" he told his wolf.

"We didn't say anything." Leo chuckled. Ben hadn't meant to reprimand his inner wolf aloud, but sometimes the damn beast was louder than his own thoughts, blowing horns and whistles to get his attention.

"She's keeping something from us," Erica cut in, erasing all humor.

Leo gently tugged on Erica's hand, pulling her back down on the sofa with him on his lap. Ben sat down beside them and placed Erica's legs over his thighs. "Do you have any ideas?"

"No, but did you see her face? It's really bad. Even worse than someone betraying us, I think."

"Let's give her some space … for now." Ben respected the hell out of Corrine and her visions, but he wasn't going to allow her or anyone else to jeopardize Erica's safety. If what she saw concerned his woman, he'd drag it out of her if he had to. No sense in telling said woman that, however, and he was fairly certain about where Corinne's loyalties lay after what she had told them earlier and he wanted to know more. "Tell us about your time with her."

"Well, you know she was my *Quenya*, my nanny…"

Erica fondly described her childhood moments with Corrine, but when she got up to the part about her parents' murder, his heart bled for his pixie as well as for Corinne. There was so much more he needed to know, like what was done to her in captivity. He wanted every mother-fucking participant's name and their role so that he knew just how much to torture each and every one of them. His own earlier blood lust was nothing compared to what he felt now. Leo's angry and heartbroken face must have mirrored his own.

Ben wanted to kick himself now though for making Erica relive the moment for the second time that day, despite the fact that he was pretty sure—based on her nightmare—that she constantly relived her horrid past every time she tried to sleep. No more, no more for her today. He wiped her tears away and leaned forward to kiss her forehead.

"Why don't we go rest in one of the rooms upstairs before the pack meeting tonight?" Leo suggested, hugging Erica close. "I am going to go pull the Alpha aside first and see if he has any ideas about a possibly disgruntled pack member."

"What if it's Gabe?" Erica asked with a hiccup.

"Gabe would never betray his pack. He's a man of honor and has way too much pride in what he's built here," Leo explained. "The expression on his face earlier told me everything I needed to know. Gabe would rather die than surrender to anyone. And Alefric requesting his surrender and sending a Fae flunky to his house, no less, was an extremely foolish miscalculation on his part. No, he's almost as thirsty for that bastard's blood as we are now."

Ben agreed. Nevertheless, everyone was suspect until this was all over, everyone except for his brother and Erica of course. Ben stood up and held his hand out for Erica to take. "Let's get you upstairs, my little pixie."

Erica smiled up at him, though her smile did not quite reach her watery eyes, and took his hand. When she stood up, she looked as pale as Corrine had looked when she had her vision. "What is it, love?"

"I think I know what Corrine may have been keeping from us." Erica put her hand on her chest. "The dove … I need to know if it uttered a cry in her vision. Oh gods!"

"So what if it did?" Erica remained silent. Ben took both her hands in his. Leo wrapped an arm around her waist from behind. "Erica, what does it mean if she heard it cry?"

"Death. It means someone is going to die."

Chapter Twelve

Leo's heart continued to break for his mate. Corrine's vision took an added toll on Erica after everything that she had already been through. Ben finally managed to get her upstairs to rest while Leo went in search of his Alpha to get a better reading on this traitor business.

He was just walking up to Gabe's office when he heard the end of the Alpha's conversation with his Beta, Donovan.

"Did you find the bastard's trail and leave him at the portal to their world?" Gabe asked gruffly, obviously still furious that Alefric would dare to insult his honor with such a demand of surrender.

"I did, Alpha. I left the messenger … and his parts where the scent trail ended. I can only assume that is where they sent him through the Veil. I'll go back out and see if they've retrieved him or he's turned to ash by now. Perhaps I can pick up a second scent trail."

"Very good. Take one of the others with you just to be safe, though." Gabe then looked up to see Leo standing by the doorway and motioned him forward to sit down at the large desk. "I don't want any wolf out in those woods alone until we get this resolved."

Donovan nodded at Gabe and left the room without another word. Leo couldn't help but wonder about the quiet Beta. Donavan had only been with the pack for about five years now. He'd come from some overly crowded pack up in northern Alberta, and once he'd taken his oath to Gabe, he'd risen through the ranks pretty quickly. As Enforcers, Leo and Ben didn't have much time for socializing, so they didn't know him too well, but he liked the guy. He'd proven himself a strong wolf and a competent Beta, and Leo was glad Gabe had the support.

"Corrine had another vision after you left," Leo said quietly. "She thinks that someone from within is going to betray the pack."

"Fuck." Gabe cursed under his breath and ran a hand through his thick, blonde hair. "This couldn't come at a worse time. We've admitted almost a dozen new males into the pack in the last six months. It could be any one of them!"

"I know. We'll just have to be very tight-lipped from now on about our tactics. I imagine that the false King has gotten our message by now and he can't be too happy."

The more Leo thought about Alefric's message, the more he suspected that a war was exactly what he wanted rather than peace with their pack. From Erica's recollection of the day her family had been killed, it sounded like the man was dead-set on subjugating all shifters. He wanted more than just Erica and would never declare a truce with the pack, even if they had given her up willingly. Albeit, giving her up would have been over his and Ben's dead body after they massacred all those who attempted to surrender her in the first place. In the end, and not surprisingly, Alefric would betray them all. Perhaps, Leo considered, they could find a way to use his own deceitfulness and arrogance against him to win this war.

"I can see the wheels turning in your head, friend. Why not go rest with your mate and your brother? You can tell me what ideas you've come up with when you get it sorted out. It usually takes you a few hours once you get that look on your face." Gabe smiled and pushed his own chair back to stand. "I'm going to go and make sure that Corrine is all right. Those visions can take a lot out of her."

****

Corrine sat in her favorite chair out by the big elm tree in the back of the estate and thought about what she'd seen in her vision that afternoon. Deep down, she'd already had a feeling that none of them would escape this war without great loss, but knowing still didn't make the thought of bearing that kind of pain any less daunting.

"What are you doing out here all by yourself, Cor? You'll freeze." Gabe took his jacket off and wrapped it around her shoulders and then sat down next to her on the wicker loveseat.

"I won't freeze any more than you will, wolf," she said with a sigh, resting her head on his shoulder, "but I appreciate your care."

"Are you all right? Leo told me that you'd had another vision after I left—a bad one." Gabe put his arm around her and gathered her close to share his warmth.

"It was bad," she whispered. "I'm afraid this war with my people will cost us more than we ever thought. You have to promise me, Gabe, that no matter what happens, you must protect Princess Eyrica at all costs. The future of both of our races will be dependent upon her survival."

"I will, Corrine. I give you my word. I swear it." Gabe leaned in to kiss the crown of her long, strawberry blonde hair. "We will protect her together, you and I."

Corrine was glad that Gabe could not see the sad smile that crossed her face at his words. She'd been with this pack for over a decade, and this had truly felt like home to her now. The courageous Alpha meant more to her than she'd ever admitted, even to herself. But she'd taken an oath to protect her Queen and the royal family and that was an oath she'd uphold even if she had to walk into the very depths of hell to do it.

Chapter Thirteen

"Why don't I draw you a nice hot bath to help you relax?" Ben suggested to Erica as soon as Leo left to seek out Gabe. The Alpha was gracious enough to give up his room, a large master bedroom with a king-sized bed and an en-suite bathroom. Both the bathtub and the shower were large enough to fit at least three people comfortably. *Perhaps Gabe prepared for his own hopeful future,* he thought.

"Only if you join me," Erica pleaded. There was no trace of seductive humor in her voice. "I don't want to be alone right now."

"Come here, love." He beckoned, holding out his hand for her to take. When she reached him, he enfolded her in his arms and whispered in her ear, "You don't have to be alone ever again. We've got you."

When he released her, he gently led her by the hand into the bathroom. He sat on the edge of the tub and started the water. Once the temperature was to his liking, he stood up, firmly cupped Erica's cheeks, and kissed her slowly, deeply. Then he let his hands trail gently down her sides until they reached the hem of her shirt. Only then did he break apart from their kiss, just long enough to lift her shirt over her head. He deftly removed her bra, unzipping her jeans as well as his own before he needed to release her lips once again. If he got to love her for a thousand lifetimes, he'd still never tire of the taste of her sweet berry-flavored lips.

Ben steadily held her gaze as he dropped to his knees in front of her to remove her shoes and socks and then finally her jeans and underwear. He could not resist inhaling the sweet and tangy scent of her arousal. He spread her pussy lips with his thumbs and flicked his tongue over her clit. One of Erica's hands grabbed onto his shoulder for balance, while the other fisted in his hair. She panted heavily as he continued to tease her little bundle of nerves.

As much as he relished in the taste of her, this was not the time to tease. He needed her, to feel himself inside of her while shutting all the danger looming over them out.

He stood abruptly, lifted Erica to straddle his waist, and stepped into the tub. As soon as he sat down, she took him inside of her, both of them moaning loudly at the contact. His love was just as desperate for him as he was for her. Their lips and tongues collided once again as she rode him hard. The sounds of the faucet still running and water sloshing to their fast paced rhythm intermingled with their loud moans and heavy breathing.

Ben fit so easily with her. Fulfillment and aching all wrapped up in one neat little exhilarating package. He'd be damned if he would be denied a lifetime of this. *Fuck that!* His wolf echoed. *Ours forever!*

He grabbed her hips and pushed up hard and fast as Erica pushed down with equal fervor. They broke their kiss again to stare sat each other, but not for long. Erica's eyes rolled back, forcing her to close them. He felt her walls tighten even further, squeezing, urging him to come with her. When she threw her head back, he buried his face in the crook of her neck and wrapped his arms tightly around her.

Ignoring the sound of the door quietly opening and closing—he knew his brother was now their audience—Ben let go in sync with Erica. His loud groan would surely have been heard throughout the house had it not been muffled by Erica's neck. His sexy pixie, however, was not so quiet. The echo of her desperate cries must have resonated at least down the hallway.

Perhaps everyone was still downstairs, but either way, he couldn't bring himself to care after what the two of them just shared.

He held her tightly for a few moments more, knowing that she needed Leo, too. It was Ben's turn now to relax and just admire the view.

****

Leo stepped into the bathroom and closed the door, not able to take his eyes from the beauty before him. His mate had her head thrown back, an expression of sheer rapture on her face as she found her pleasure, and the sounds of her passion were the sweetest music to his ears.

He stepped up to the bath and turned off the running water before there was even more of it on the floor. He understood very well how his brother hadn't noticed the mess.

"Oh crap, the water," Ben said once he'd noticed the sloshing sound of Leo's steps.

"Yes, brother, seems you were seduced by a mermaid. I can see how you'd lose track of the rest of the world." Leo smiled down at Erica as he cupped her cheek with his hand and leaned in for a gentle kiss. "How are you feeling, love?"

"Better now that you're here as well." Erica kissed him back with a heat that had him growling low in the back of his throat.

"Stand up, little one," Leo ordered as he took a step back and watched the water slip off of her perfect, creamy curves.

He held out his hand to her, and when she accepted it, he helped her step out of the tub and onto the warm tile.

"Oh, you're in for it now, pixie. I've seen that

look before." Ben laughed as he sat back in the tub with a sigh.

Leo tried not to smile when their mate's eyes opened a little wider in concern, but he wanted to keep her off balance for this. They'd both enjoy it more.

"Now, undress me."

"Yes, sir." Erica winked at him and moved her hands to pull his t-shirt up and over his head, her fingers then trailing down to tease over his stomach muscles.

"No teasing, Erica. Continue," he commanded her in his most business-like voice, but damn if her soft little hands didn't undo him when she unfastened the button on his jeans and slowly slid down the zipper. Leo felt Erica hesitate. His pixie wanted to play, but one stern look from him finally made her finish removing his pants and tossing them to the side.

"Very good, baby," Leo growled in her ear. He then took her hand and led her to the vanity counter, turned her around so that she was looking at herself in the mirror, and he positioned her hands flat on the counter. "Now don't move those hands, understand?"

Erica nodded in agreement while biting down on her lip. He could smell how turned on she was by his game. Ben got out of the tub, and Leo took a few steps back to stand by his brother to admire her, leaning there in all her glory. He could see her watching him and Ben in the mirror. Leo stepped forward to urge her feet farther apart. He heard his brother groan at what must be a spectacular view. Leo then ran his hands up the inside of her thighs until his fingers brushed her soaked folds that were beckoning to him.

"Damn, baby, you're so wet," he whispered in her ear before nibbling along her soft neck. "I think you like our little game, don't you?"

He rewarded her for her agreement by sliding his

hand around her pelvis and slowly pushing his fingers deep into her pussy. He could not resist grinding his painfully hard cock against her ass. Her panting and keening as she tried to move on his fingers were enough to make him almost lose control, but he was enjoying himself too much to stop, so he brought his free hand down quick and hard across her generous ass.

"Behave now, baby. You'll take what I give you." Leo felt her pussy spasm at the snap of pain to her ass, and he couldn't help but admire the bloom of his handprint against her pale flesh. Clearly they would have to explore this more. Their little mate was turning out to be chock full of lovely surprises.

He slowly pulled out his fingers, leaving one to spread her honey all over her swollen clit. Leo took his cock and brought the tip down to the sweet haven that he was desperate to possess. Erica was so warm and wet, he couldn't hold back from entering her pussy in one long thrust. He could feel her rippling around his flesh as he rubbed circles around her clit, and when he felt her tighten, he knew she was about to come. Leo didn't want to get left behind, so he sped up, pumping furiously into her, and when he met her frantic eyes in the mirror he released her clit and grabbed onto her hips with both hands.

"Come all over my cock, baby. Do it now!" He growled still looking into her eyes until she keened out again and threw her head back as she came in a glorious display. Leo ground himself into her as deep as he could go and groaned as he found his release deep inside his mate.

****

Erica awoke almost silently, fighting the urge to run. She forced herself to breathe through the hysteria that swelled within her until she could think clearly. After such a wonderfully orgasmic end to the evening, waking in the early hours of the next day from a nightmare as hellish as the one she'd just experienced was more than just a rude awakening. It was downright cruel.

She had been standing alone in a darkened field. The sun had set, the air felt cool, and nothing looked familiar. She spun in a slow circle, desperate for a hint of her location, but there was nothing but for the ever-lengthening shadows of the forest that surrounded the field. Her heart began to pound hard within her chest, and her breathing sounded harsh to her own ears.

"Eyrica."

Erica spun in the direction of the whispered voice, almost tumbling to the ground in her haste, but there had been no one there.

"Eyrica."

She spun again. The voice was louder this time, and it came from a different direction. Her fear and anxiety kept building within her. Despite the years since she had heard it, she knew the voice belonged to her mother.

"Eyrica."

For the third time Erica spun, looking for her mother, and finding nothing and no one there. Tears streamed down her face as she turned in tight circles, desperately trying to find her mother, knowing that she was there with her, but somehow out of reach. From the corner of her eye, a small movement had her whirling to her right. A dove flew directly at her, a message in its claws, and although it was too high to make out the markings on the paper, the red of the blood used to pen the message was clear to see.

It had been the dove's high-pitched cries, loud and consistent as it flew, that caused Erica to wake up from her dream. She resisted the urge to clamber from the bed and run, but barely. Erica had never been gifted with such a vision, and she knew that what she saw mirrored that which Corrine had witnessed earlier. She also knew the sound could mean only one thing. Death was coming, and it would not be denied.

But who? Corrine had been shown more than she had told them, of that Erica was certain. Corinne had been shaken when she had come out of the vision, but it was the panic with a strong edge of fear in her eyes that told Erica that her former nanny had been rocked by what she had seen. Whomever death was coming for, their passing would be significant, and it left her stumped as to why the vision had been revealed to her when she did not possess the seer gift.

Erica began to think about the possibilities. If it were Corrine that was to die, the aftermath of that could potentially be quite catastrophic. It was hard to miss the connection between her *Quenya* and the Alpha wolf, not to mention how greatly the loss would affect Erica.

Gabe would lead his pack to war, Erica standing right beside him, urging those still loyal to her and her family to stand with her. The effects and reach of the battle to come would no doubt be felt in both realms for a long time. If Gabe is the one meant to die, the repercussions of his death would also be felt on both sides of the Veil.

Then, of course, what if *she* was the one meant to die? Alefric's rule might never be overthrown, and innocents of the entire Elven realm and beyond the Veil would continue to suffer or be killed under his unjust reign. On this side of the Veil, her mates would mourn her death, but they and the pack might yet survive the war although continuous wars between the two factions seemed inevitable

The outcome that Erica feared the most was that Corrine had foreseen the death of one or both of her mates. If Leo or Ben were killed by Alefric and his men, Erica would be unstoppable in her grief. She was a healer for her kind, someone who could channel and focus the very life energy of a person to heal them, or use the abundance of healing energy within herself. She could also use her powers defensively and offensively as an electrically charged shield or a force she could throw out in front of her. Erica could usually control the strength of the emittance, unless her focus was on healing herself or others or, as she unfortunately demonstrated to Leo and Ben, when her defenses were a side effect from her nightmares. If she were inconsolable, however, completely bereft and devoid of logic or reasoning as any woman would be when faced with the murder of her mates, she may very well be able to use that life force as a weapon. Could this have been what Corrine foresaw? That the only way to stop Alefric was to become a weapon?

No, that would be unnatural!

But then the idea began to nag at her. *Use the ability to draw a person's life force as a weapon.* The thought went round and round in her head for a while. It was forbidden to use her healing abilities for anything other than to heal, but Erica figured the alternative of seeing that prick Alefric ruling over her people and going to war with a race of shifters simply because he believed them inferior to him might just be the exception. Not to mention that even the thought of one or both of her mates being killed had her already half-crazed.

If she was going to do this, then she needed to get close to Alefric. She would need to start easing his life force from him, not wanting to startle him into action before she could do what needed to be done. He needed to feel confident and in control, and that there was no threat to him until it was too late. And that meant confronting him alone.

And if she was going to do this, then she needed to do it when Leo and Ben were unable to stop her. Tears welled at the thought of leaving them. She felt her heart breaking within her.

Can I do this?

She had to. This could very well be their only chance.

Chapter Fourteen

Closing her eyes, Erica drew the healing energy within her to the fore, molding it into the form she needed to send her mates into a deeper sleep. She knew that if she attempted to leave, they would notice immediately and stop her. With a heavy heart, Erica pushed the energy from her. The light that came from within her was unavoidable, and she heard both her mates wake and sit up beside her.

"What the hell?" Leo mumbled. Erica knew he was already feeling and most likely trying to fight the effects. It would be in vain.

"Erica?" Ben asked gently at the same time, his eyes wide before both of them surrendered to the effects of the energy she fed them. They fell back onto the mattress, caught in a deep sleep.

Sobbing quietly, Erica scrambled off the bed. She dragged on her clothes and secured her sheathed sword to her back, all the time avoiding looking at her men. Her resolve was weak where they were concerned, and she knew that if she allowed her gaze to linger she would not have the courage to do what was needed. Only when she was dressed did she come back to the bed. Wiping the tears from her face, she leaned in and pressed a kiss to Ben's lips before circling the bed to kiss Leo. As goodbyes went, it was pretty damn pathetic, but it was all she could allow.

"Forgive me, my loves," she whispered from the doorway. Then she stepped into the hallway. Despite the fact that the house was quiet, Erica knew there would no doubt be men stationed on guard around it, especially considering the message Alefric had sent that afternoon.

Walking quietly downstairs, Erica stepped into the almost deserted kitchen. Only one wolf sat at the counter, drinking a steaming cup of coffee.

"Donovan, what's keeping you up at night?" Erica stepped into the kitchen but stood so that she was between him and the back door.

Donovan looked at her with curiosity. "Hell, princess, there's a whole lot of shit that keeps me awake at night. But what is driving my curiosity at the moment is wondering if you think you really stand a chance to get out that door, before I'm on you."

Erica held the man's gaze. People had been attempting to intimidate her most of her life, and she had yet to allow anyone to succeed. "Oh, I'd give myself a fair chance, Beta. And just because we're having a conversation, and asking and answering questions nice and friendly like, I feel the need to ask, why would you care? If my intention after walking into the kitchen tonight was to in fact go out that door, why would you feel like you needed to stop me?"

Erica was mildly surprised at his hate-filled sneer. "So the princess is going to run. What a fucking surprise. Let me guess, you're going to run as far and as fast as your fucking legs can carry you from the war that is coming." Donovan suddenly stood up, so fast the chair he'd been sitting on almost fell over, and Erica stepped back a couple of steps, her hand automatically sliding to the hilt of her sword. "Normally, I wouldn't give a shit what you or your fucking kind do, but when you think to put me and mine in danger because you are a spineless bitch with no fucking sense of what is right, then yeah, I sure as shit am going to stop you."

Unfazed by Donovan's tirade, Erica stared at him, her face devoid of all emotion. "Where does your allegiance lie, Donovan? Are you loyal to Gabe?"

Erica saw a slight flicker of guilt in his eyes, and

she knew immediately that Donovan was the traitor. She pulled her sword and brought it in front of her as Donovan's eyes began to shimmer, his wolf close to the surface. It was really fucking ironic that in her bid to escape the house and get to Alefric to, she hoped, save the day would be thwarted by the fact that she had stumbled across the traitor.

"It surprises the shit out me that despite your obvious hatred of … how did you put it? *My kind?* You would align yourself with Alefric and his followers."

Rage filled Donovan's expression, and Erica took another step back, wanting to put more distance between them. "I would never align myself with that narcissistic bastard. You ask me who I am loyal to? My family! My mate and my brother, first and foremost. No one, not even Gabe or the pack I have sworn fealty to, takes precedence over them."

Erica stared into his eyes for a moment gauging his sincerity. The hatred he had for Alefric was clear. "Then if that is the case, show me where you took the messenger. Leo told me that you returned him to the Fae, so you must know where a portal through the Veil is. Take me there and I promise you, I will end Alefric."

Shock or some other emotion Erica couldn't quite name flittered across the Beta's face. "You want to go back across the Veil? Alefric wants you dead, but you want to go back there?"

Erica sighed as she re-sheathed her sword. "Yeah, I know, I'm a complicated woman. I have a plan, one that will hopefully end with Alefric frying in hell like he should. But in order for me to execute this plan, I have to go back and face him. Alone."

Donovan seemed to be weighing up her sincerity, and no doubt assessing whether or not she spoke the truth. "It's not far. I'll take you."

When they exited the house, Donovan spoke with the guards that walked the perimeter of the property. The further they got from the house, the more her heart broke. She took deep breaths, resisting the need to turn and run back to her mates, and fighting the urge to burst into tears when she certainly did not have time for them. They would do her no good right now anyway.

"Here," Donovan suddenly said, pointing to a slight opening between two large rocks protruding from a cliff wall.

Had Erica not been lost in her own pain and grief at leaving, she would have been able to feel the faint energy emanating from the break in the Veil that allowed transition between the realms, if one knew how to manipulate the energy properly. Perhaps this was where Corrine had come through all those years ago.

Erica walked towards the break, but turned before she stepped through. Despite her best efforts, tears slipped freely down her cheeks. "I know that you don't owe me anything." Her voice was hoarse, pain and loss clear in her tone. "But I have one favor to ask of you. Will you hear it?"

Confusion clear on his face, Donovan nodded.

"If what I am about to do succeeds, then I will be back to beg my mates for forgiveness at having done this on my own. But if I fail, and I am unable to kill Alefric, then could you please give Leo and Ben this message. Tell them that although I have loved them for just a short time, the depth of my love could not be deeper. Had I known them all my life, and we had been blessed with multiple lifetimes, our bond would be as true. Tell them that they have my heart, and it will beat with theirs for the rest of time."

Donovan's face softened, then flooded with guilt.

He seemed to be wrestling with an inner torment that she was not privy to, but she was beyond caring. Donovan would give her mates her message. She had to believe that. Turning, she quickly wove the Elven sigils in the air that unlocked the bridge and allowed her through the Veil. As she entered into the maelstrom that existed between the two realms, she spun one last time to lay eyes on the earth realm. She saw Donovan reaching out to her, his face filled with regret, and he was shouting something she couldn't make out. Then, everything went black as she made the transition through the Veil finding herself atop the bridge that lay on the other side.

****

"God-fucking-damn it!" Donovan roared as Erica disappeared from sight. He stepped between the rocks, standing in the exact place she had just been, and there was nothing there. Just rock on three sides of him. "Fuck!" He yelled and punched the wall in front of him a few times just for good measure.

How did everything get so fucked up so quickly? He'd thought he had everything all figured out. The world was black and white and there was no gray, but his brother had always told him that he needed to see the gray once in a while to truly get the bigger picture. Jason had always been the one who saw what was really going on. And this was just another example of Donovan only seeing what he wanted.

He thought he'd understood how the Fae worked. He was a firm believer in understanding every nuance of his enemy, but this one, Erica, she was different. She headed into the realm knowing that it would most likely mean her death. She was going to face Alefric, the prick who thought he had Donovan's balls on the chopping block, and because that Fae fucker had Jason and April hostage, that was pretty much true. He knew his brother and their mate would be as good as dead should Donovan not do as the False King demanded. But Alefric wouldn't *see* this coming. He would just assume Donovan had done what he had been tasked to do: deliver the princess into the Elven realm and tell no one.

Hearing Erica talk about her love for Leo and Ben, two men Donovan had grown to like and respect in the last several years, had finally snapped him out of the selfish rhetoric that it was all about him, and he *finally* saw the bigger picture. Jason would be fucking furious if he knew Donovan had been willing to sacrifice an innocent woman for him, and although he had yet to meet April, he instinctively knew his mate wouldn't be overly happy with him either.

Donovan spun from the rock and leaped into the air, shifting as he went. He landed on all fours and started sprinting back to Gabe's house. He was going to have to come clean with Gabe, and that would mean exile from the pack if he was lucky, but more than likely it would mean his death. Donovan thought about how Leo and Ben would react when they found out he had let their mate simply walk into the lion's den, and suddenly death sounded like it would be the better deal than what the two Enforcers could do to him.

Chapter Fifteen

Ben let out a loud roar as he struggled for the umpteenth time to open his eyes. At least, his angry roars were no longer just in his head. He actually heard himself this time. The feeling in his arms was starting to come back as well.

"Relax, Ben," he heard his brother say.

"Relax? *Relax?* How the fuck am I supposed to … Erica… she…" Ben choked on a sob, still struggling to get his eyes open. "Why the fuck are you so calm?"

"I'm pissed," Leo said coolly. "And I am scared shitless," he added in a monotone. "And I feel so fucking helpless right now that I may start punching things as soon as I am able just for the fuck of it. I feel anything but calm, brother," he concluded through gritted teeth. "I discovered that if you struggle less, whatever she did to us wears off quicker."

Ben took Leo's advice and relaxed his breathing and calmed his heart rate. Within minutes, he was able to open up his eyes. The ability to turn his neck came next. Leo's head was turned in his direction when Ben turned to look at him, a blank expression on his face, except for his eyes. His eyes were blazing. His brother was definitely not calm at all.

Leo regained the ability to move his legs first, but when he tried to stand, his legs gave out and finally he lost his collected composure. He slumped back down on the bed, his fists banging the mattress on the way down. "How the fuck could she do this to us? What in the hell was she thinking? How could she go off by herself knowing what it would do to us if she wasn't successful?" Leo's wolf came close to the surface, eyes glowing, fangs dropping, and almost immediately, he shot up off the bed, Erica's paralytic sleep spell dissolved.

Ben figured that was the key to the final step and let his own wolf come to the surface and then the pair of them ran out of that room like hell itself was chasing them.

One of the guards, Roderick, met them at the bottom of the stairs. "What has happened?"

"Where are Gabe and Donovan?" Leo asked impatiently.

"Leo, calm down and tell me what's got you both so frantic."

"Donovan took the Fae messenger to the gate through the Veil. We need him to show us where it is right now! Now tell me where the hell he is before I rip your motherfucking head off."

"Erica's gone," Ben added.

"Gone? What the hell do you mean she is gone?" Roderick seemed affronted, like Erica being missing was a personal insult to him. Ben would help Leo decapitate him in a minute if he didn't give them some information or get the fuck out of their way. "I would have known if someone broke into—"

"That stubborn child left on her own," said Corrine as she walked down the hallway dressed in a long silk robe. "Sleeping death, I take it?"

Ben turned his anger on Corrine. "You knew she would do this? You knew and you let her—"

"Of course not, you foolish wolf!" she snapped. "I did not foresee her doing this completely alone, just that she was the one most likely meant to kill Alefric. This kind of sleeping spell, well, it leaves a trace of magic behind. Those who know what to look for can see it and I can see it in both of you, your eyes and in your slower gait, but you should be fine soon. I fear it must have taken a toll on Erica as well. She has gone beyond the Veil still weakened. I would have stopped her if I knew."

"Fuck!" Ben roared right before he punched a hole through Gabe's wall. Fortunately for Roderick, he had the good sense to step out of the way.

"I took her to the entrance." Donovan stood in the hallway, a fuming Gabe by his side. "I took her, and I watched her go through."

"Why would you do that?" Leo asked, back to his deadly calm self.

"She asked me to. I'm sorry. By the time I realized … it was too late." Donovan bowed his head in shame.

Ben charged at Donovan. No one attempted to stop him, not even some of the other guards who had slowly started to gather around them. And when Ben's hands were firmly wrapped around Donovan's throat, he asked him through gritted teeth, "You're the traitor?"

"I had no choice." A tear escaped Donovan.

"There is always a choice!" Ben roared in his face.

"He has Jason and April, Ben."

"Let him tell you the whole story," Gabe ordered, resting his hand on Ben's forearm. "We will save your mate. I swear it. You may do what you will to him afterward, as is your right, but hear him first. He came to me just now of his own accord to confess everything."

Ben looked up at Gabe to see the passion and sincerity of his words. And he did not miss the fact that Gabe's eyes had strayed to where Corrine stood. His Alpha no doubt meant the vow that he had spoken.

"We are wasting time," Leo barked. "Let him lead us to the opening and he can tell us along the way."

Ben reluctantly let go of Donovan's throat.

"That's fine. We can snap his neck later and leave him there."

Reflexively, Donovan's hands shot up to his throat when Ben released him, massaging away the ache. Hoarsely, he informed them, "I can lead you there, but I don't know how to enter."

"But I do," Corinne informed. "I can lead a whole damn army in there."

Gabe nodded. "Then that's what we'll bring—a whole damn army. We'll bring the fight to them. Tonight!"

Chapter Sixteen

Leo looked once again at the traitor, Donovan, as he led them to the site of Erica's crossing in the direction of the clearing out by the old hunting lodge. He was shocked that it had been their Beta who'd betrayed them, and though his first instinct was along the same lines as Ben's—to kill him outright for endangering his own mate—his brain knew they needed answers first.

"Tell us, Donovan, where is your brother?"

"I wondered why I hadn't seen him in two days," Gabe remarked in between murmuring instructions to the other wolves at his side.

Leo knew that Gabe would be arranging for all the other Alphas in the area to send their own warriors to join them across the Veil. After all, this entire power play of Alefric's was designed to secure the throne with his own people while starting the enslavement of everyone else. This concerned all shifters everywhere, but that didn't stop the shock that ran through Leo when Gabe finally instructed Roderick to call the two other shifter groups that lived nearby. Their wolf pack had always been on friendly terms with the bear and cat shifters who lived on Vancouver Island, but nevertheless, they had never called to ask them for assistance in anything. This impending battle was getting more interesting by the minute. Furthermore, the Fae would never suspect shifters other than the wolves, since they were the ones Alefric had challenged, to be called to arms, and therefore, it would be a great advantage for them.

"He's been missing since the night before Ben and Leo found Erica," Donovan told them. "After the pack meeting, Jason called me. He was supposed to bring April back to the house to meet me within the hour, but they never arrived. Jason later left me a voicemail letting me know that he went back out on patrol after he learned that our mate's friend went missing. That was the last I heard from him." Donovan had stopped walking to tell his side of the story, but by the look on his face, the wolf was barely keeping it together at the thought of how long his brother and mate had been in the hands of the Fae. "The King's guard, Kheelan, called me from Jason's phone saying that he had both of them and if I didn't follow their instructions then he would kill them."

All of the wolves stopped when Donovan fell to his knees in agony, and Leo knew that he would have made the same decision if it had been Ben and Erica in danger.

"I'm so sorry, Alpha. I deserve worse than death for betraying you all," the man sobbed, "but they are my heart and I could not let them go. Not when there was something I could do to save them. Once they were safe, it was always my intention to find a way through the Veil and kill that son of a bitch."

Gabe helped the other wolf to his feet and pulled him into an embrace. Leo could no longer feel any hostility coming from any members of their pack. Anyone who was mated had forgiven him already.

"Come, show us where Erica passed though, Donovan. Then we will all go and retrieve the rest of our pack, including your brother and mate." Gabe grabbed Corrine's hand tightly as he led their group behind the broken wolf.

Leo was still picking up Erica's scent when they finally made it to a large clearing, adjacent to a rock face. When Donovan finally stopped in front of the stone, Leo's wolf began to panic. That was where Erica's scent abruptly ended. Obviously, this was the point of her crossing. He looked towards his brother and he knew that

Ben would charge across into any possible scenario if it meant going after their mate, but they all needed to be smart about this. Corrine was the only one who really knew what lay on the other side of this portal. They could end up directly in the lap of the enemy for all these wolves knew, and that wouldn't help any of their loved ones.

"Where does this lead to in the Fae realm, Corrine?" Leo asked as he ran his hand along the solid stone. It was almost unbelievable to imagine that it led to another magical place.

"This is the same portal that I came though when I escaped Alefric's dungeons. It emerges in the forest about a half day's walk from the palace. It should be safe when we send you through."

"Leo, Ben, and Donovan, I know you will want to go through right away, but I will need you to do some recon and not immediately storm the palace. I don't need you three getting yourselves killed because I gotta tell you, right now your best chance is to think like soldiers, not mates. That's an order," Gabe commanded before turning to one of his guards. "Roderick, what do you have for me?"

The other wolf had been on his cell phone the entire time since Donovan had started his tale. Leo knew that the pack house must be a flurry of chaos at the moment, trying to coordinate getting in touch with the rest of the local wolves, not to mention the bear clan and the cougars on the Island.

"Alpha, our wolves are coming directly here, and the cougar Alpha is already on his way with about fifty men. They chartered a flight so they should be here within the hour. The bears aren't fond of flying so they're—about a hundred of them—taking the ferry. I have no idea where we're going to fit all those giants!"

Roderick rubbed his forehead as though the thought of how to accommodate all of the extra people was giving him a headache.

"That should give us plenty of men to hit the palace. Some of the most skilled and loyal of the original Royal Guard were executed for treason when they wouldn't support Alefric's claim on the throne," Corrine explained as she stepped forward and began to write the gate sigils on the stone with her fingers. "Alefric's Royal Guard is severely lacking in my opinion."

"Just remember, Leo," Gabe said, looking pointedly at him, as if he would be the voice of reason even though he had so much at stake, "no one does anything stupid. We don't want to alert the scum to our attack. We don't even know if Erica is with Alefric yet. She may still be planning *her* attack. Get the intel and pull back to the gate until we join you."

Gabe is right, Leo thought. If this was going to work, they needed to take the False King completely unawares and end his reign permanently.

Chapter Seventeen

Erica shook off the remnants of disorientation that came when one traveled across the bridge beyond the Veil. She dropped to her hands and knees and took three deep breaths, her equilibrium slowly returning with each one. Finally, pushing away the cloud of nausea that had settled over her, she stood up and looked at the forest around her.

The trees in the Elven realm were large, standing straight and tall, much like the giant pine trees Leo and Ben had pointed out on their journey to Gabe's. Erica had to breathe through the pain that accompanied the thought of her mates. If she were to dwell on them, she would crumble. She had a job to do, and she was going to have to stay strong to get it done.

Standing tall and throwing back her shoulders, she started walking in the direction of the palace. The day was just coming to an end here. The sun was high in the sky and the air warm, gently scented with the earthy aroma of the forest she had loved to play in as a child. Her father would often tease her that she was more Wood Elf than Fae. The memories of her father steeled her resolve once again, and she hastened her steps.

She figured she wouldn't have to go far before she was met by Alefric's guard. He would have been alerted to the bridge opening by now, and since she did not attempt to hide her arrival, he'd send guards to meet whoever had entered the realm. Two hours later, she sensed movement ahead of her and stopped in a small clearing. It took all the control she possessed not to draw her blade. Waiting for capture went against everything in her, but it was all part of her plan.

Erica's skin crawled when Kheelan strode out of the trees before her, his hair pulled back, his black soulless eyes staring at her with barely constrained glee, but what really pissed her off was the fucker hadn't drawn his sword. Either he didn't see her as a threat or he had come with a full squadron. Both options had her seeing red.

"Why, Princess Eyrica," Kheelan's voice positively dripped with sarcasm, the inflection in her name slightly different as he used the Fae name she had been born with, "it does do my heart good to see you back in the Elven realm. It certainly makes it easier to hunt when the prey presents itself to me in my own forest."

Erica smiled sweetly at the asshole, knowing that it would piss him off. His narrowed eyes that were now tinged with red told her it had worked. "Well, there you go again, Kheelan, putting on airs and believing your station in life is higher than it actually is. Remember, your position is on your knees in front of your hideous King, or bent over the nearest hard surface. Being the King's fuck-buddy doesn't give you the right to claim these forests as your own."

Kheelan's face turned an interesting shade of purple. "You think you're fucking better than me, *Ittee*? My King and I know that you've been spreading your legs for those two fucking dogs, and if my eyes are correct, you actually let those mongrels claim you. Have you no fucking loyalty to your Fae heritage?"

"Loyalty?" Erica snarled. "You dare to question my loyalty in being Fae? Look in the goddamn mirror, Kheelan. You stand beside the man who killed the true King and Queen of this realm. You did his fucking dirty work every time you raised your fists to me because I refused to either fuck or marry your False King. You speak accurately when you say I have slept with two shifters, and hell yes, I let them claim me, as I fucking claimed them! They are my mates as foreseen by one of our own seers and destined for me by the Fates themselves. How dare you question my loyalty?"

Kheelan lifted his arm, and eight of Alefric's senior guards walked out of the woods and surrounded her. "Your parents were defiling our world and our people by allowing shifters to roam free. They are nothing but vermin, and if you have allowed yourself to be sullied by two of them, then it is you who has been disloyal to your lineage."

Erica turned to look around at the guards, staring each and every one of them in the eye. "Alefric killed your King and your Queen. You were their guards, and you failed them." It might have been simply wishful thinking on her behalf, but Erica thought that perhaps she saw a flicker of guilt on the faces of one or two of them.

Kheelan drew his blade and stepped closer to her. "Enough. You have come back to this realm, and I can only assume it is because you wish to speak with our King. If that is the case, then hand me your weapon."

Erica drew her blade with all the speed and skill she possessed, grinning when Kheelan stepped back. "Aw, did I scare you?"

"No," Kheelan snarled back in denial, as a few of the guards surrounding her looked like they were biting back laughter.

Erica dropped into her fighting stance, right foot back, and balanced on the balls of her feet. She held the sword in a two handed grip and sent her power into the blade, charged it with energy, making it glow an eerie blue, telling all those that surrounded her that she battled with skill and power superior to most. "Do you want me to? Scare you that is?"

She watched as Kheelan fought an internal battle

with himself. He hated that she was calling him out in front of his men, and she could tell that he was itching to engage with her. But his hesitation told her that he had orders from Alefric, and Kheelan surely feared disappointing him.

"You are the one who stepped back into this realm, Erica," Kheelan pointed out. "You came here I assume to surrender yourself to Alefric, and if that is the case, then drop your damn sword, and we will take you to the palace. You will be heavily guarded but you will get your chance to talk with him, and I have to be honest, he is curious as hell as to why you would have come back."

Erica stood up gracefully, placing her sword on the ground, and then stepping back away from it with a smile. "That is something you'll only find out when I talk with Alefric. I'm a lady who doesn't like having to repeat myself."

Kheelan walked forward and picked up her sword. As he stood up, he moved with a speed that belied his size and swung the back of his hand across her mouth. Erica's head snapped sideways and she almost dropped to her knees, but fought to keep her feet firmly beneath her, not wanting to give him the satisfaction of seeing her fall.

Spitting blood to the forest floor, she flicked her hair off her face and looked back at him. "Let's not keep your King waiting a minute longer, shall we?"

Kheelan's gaze narrowed and he turned with a growl, calling for his men to bind her hands. Erica looked up at the two men who stepped forward to tie her hands behind her, and she knew she wasn't imagining the look of respect that flickered there. The Fae were a race that applauded strength.

Erica stood placidly, holding her arms behind her. Once she was secured, they started toward the palace. Erica felt an odd sort of calm settle over her. Today was the day she would take back what belonged to her. Alefric stood between her and the future she longed to offer her people and her mates, and if the cost of ridding her realm of Alefric and securing the safety of her mates was her life, then so be it.

Chapter Eighteen

Ben was going to be sick. He dropped to his knees as nausea overtook him. His head began to spin as his insides protested the unnatural state of atoms reshaping themselves to pass through some mystical portal, which very much resembled a bridge. Even his wolf felt it. Once they passed through the Veil, the bridge seemed to materialize out of nowhere. It was made from what looked like a thick felled tree with the inside carved out. Intricate green vines decorated both the inside and out, and some kind of translucent white mist encompassed them as they crossed on heavy footing.

He glanced over at his brother and Donovan, to see them both in pretty much the same state. Donovan was actually busy upchucking whatever he had recently eaten.

"Fuck, that hurt!" Leo groaned as he stood up on shaky legs.

Ben and Donovan grunted their agreement before they, too, stood up and tried to regain their bearings. He could only hope that when the time came for Corinne to bring through the reinforcements that they really would be able to come through undetected and have enough time to recover. Corinne had reassured them that they would enter undiscovered, but Alefric's guards could be lurking anywhere.

He wondered if the Fae experienced the same pain and discomfort when they passed through and immediately thought of Erica. His wolf growled at the thought of her suffering, even though he still felt the sting of her betrayal. He knew why she did what she did and admired her strength, but they were a trio now. He and Leo would get her back—there was no other option—and she was already forgiven, but she sure as hell would never do that to them again.

"Let's move somewhere under more cover," Leo suggested. "We're too exposed out here."

The three of them walked deeper into the large forest where there were plenty of thick trees and large rocks to hide behind if need be. Corrine had also been generous enough to provide them with a map of the terrain and pointed out the routes to avoid or take. The main goal was to reach the palace completely undetected, but if necessary they could pass through the areas where sympathizers for the true royal family lurked. She had informed them that none of them would lift a finger to help them being that they mostly just kept to themselves. Wise, since that was probably what kept them off of Alefric's radar for now. But at least none of them would report their entering the realm either, Corinne seemed confident of that.

When they spotted several guards patrolling near their location, Ben, Leo, and Donovan had to veer off course as Corinne had suggested, and just as she had predicted, the Fae folk who lurked mostly in shadows barely paid them any mind.

Ben couldn't help but marvel at the beauty of the quiet forests. It looked like something out of a fairytale with its bright green colors and strange mist, almost like on the bridge only it shimmered above rather than encompassing them. Creatures he had never seen before, large and small, poked through small openings in between bushes, branches, and rock openings to stare at them as they passed, just as curious about the three trespassers as they were of them.

One particularly large man, as large as a bear shifter in a full shift, stepped out in front of them, blocking their path. Ben, Leo, and Donovan were all pretty large men themselves, but the brute before them stood well over seven feet tall. His features were human-like, though everything from his eyes, nose, hands, etcetera, was exaggeratedly larger. And add to that, he looked like a badass biker with his raven colored, shoulder length hair pulled back in a ponytail, and what resembled tribal tattoos poked out of the sleeves of his shirt. He also sported small symbols on the sides of his neck which were indecipherable to Ben, more than likely because they were in the Elven language. And if he wasn't mistaken, the larger symbol that began from his cheekbone and ended in a swirl around his eye, appeared to have been moving.

"So much for them not interfering," Ben mumbled under his breath. The bear man looked poised for a fight.

"I am Ishaya, keeper of the forest. You must pay a toll to pass," the bear man thundered.

"Oh yeah?" Leo asked, cool sarcasm dripping from his tone as he continued. "What may be the price? But before you answer, you got a deed or something we can inspect to make sure you are said *keeper* of the forest?" He made air quotes when he said the word "keeper".

"Maybe antagonizing him isn't the best solution," Ben said. What he had in mind was more along the lines of pummeling the large man if he didn't get out of his way soon, scary looking biker dude or not. He didn't care who he had to mow down to get to their woman. Turning to face Ishaya, he asked, "What's your price? I got about eighty bucks on me, a few sticks of gum, a debit card, and my car keys, though I imagine you'd have no use for the latter two. I haven't seen any paved roads, and I tell you, finding an ATM here has been a bitch." He did not mention the fact that he had several knives and a gun strapped to his body.

Ishaya threw his head back and let out a full blown belly laugh. "I'm just messing with you. Had to see if the mate, or mates, in this case, our princess chose were worthy of her. But I think I like you two. Not quick to fists, but no pushovers either. Hard to miss the fire in your eyes. Who is the oth—"

"You've seen her?" Ben interrupted, hearing the desperation in his own voice.

"Yes. I was closer to the main road a little while ago and saw her being escorted by a few guards toward the palace."

"How did she look?" Leo demanded. When Ishaya lowered his head and fisted his hands at his side, both Leo and Ben let out simultaneous growls. Heads were going to roll, and they were all going to die.

"She had a red mark across her cheek. I couldn't … I couldn't…" The large man lowered his head again and shook it. But then he raised it and quickly added, "She held her head high and walked with dignity. She's the bravest female I know. We will not sit idly by anymore as the scum King tears apart our lands."

Donovan, who remained silent up until that point, turned to Leo and Ben, a determined look on his face, and asked, "Neither of you had planned to come here just for intel, did you?"

"No," Ben and Leo said in unison. Ben continued, "We're not going anywhere without her." He then turned to Ishaya. "We need your help, big guy. For Erica, for your people, we can't take the chance of him hurting our mate and us not … not getting to her in time." Ben took a deep breath, trying to chase away the unacceptable scenarios. He produced the map that Corinne had given them and pointed out the location from where they had entered the Veil. "We need someone to go there and let our Alpha know as much information as you can give him, about the guards, their patrol patterns, and the best way to get into the palace without being spotted."

"We have secret caves and tunnels that only forest folk know of. We keep them carefully hidden from the guards. Even the King and Queen themselves were unaware of some of them." He then explained how Erica, as a young child had stumbled upon one of them and used it to sneak out to come play with Ishaya and the forest folk.

Ishaya easily agreed to help them and began barking out orders to someone they couldn't see, until that is ten more men, some larger than Ishaya even, had stepped out of hiding, followed by several other, much smaller forest folk, and several Fae. One of the bear looking men headed straight in the direction that Ben, Leo, and Donovan had come from. He would apparently be the messenger. The three of them were then led to one of these secret caves. That would be their way in, their way to Erica.

When they entered, Donovan turned toward Ishaya. "Have you seen any other wolves? One who looks like me, but just slightly taller with lighter hair? A girl was with him. A human girl."

Ishaya tilted his head to the side. "Yes. I saw them a few days ago. They were being dragged to the palace."

It was Donovan's turn to growl now. Ben couldn't help but feel sorry for him despite what he had done. In all fairness, however, Erica would have found her way here with or without his help, even if she had to go through Donovan to do it.

"Wait a moment, a human girl, you say?" Ishaya

asked. When Donovan nodded, a cryptic "Hmm," was all the large man added before leaving the three of them alone in the cave. Ben wondered what that was all about, but they had no time to decipher Ishaya's meaning now.

"We split up when we get there," Leo said to Donovan. "Ben and I will go find Erica while you go locate your girl and brother. Don't do anything stupid, Donovan, you understand me?"

Donovan nodded.

Leo continued. "You find them and free them if you can without attracting attention. If you can't, then recon, and assume lookout position."

"What is it, Donovan?" Ben asked when Donovan suddenly stopped walking.

"Erica—she asked me to pass along a message to both of you … in case…"

"She can give it us herself," Ben snapped. The idea that there was even a remote chance of never seeing her again made him sick to his stomach. He didn't want to hear a parting message. He looked over at Leo, who seemed to be struggling with the same thoughts."

"Just know that she loves you and the decision to leave you was very difficult for her."

Ben already knew that. It would have killed him to leave her behind, especially if he thought he may never see her again. "We know that."

The three of them picked up the pace, making some more plans until they got close enough to the palace to split up.

It was time to get their pixie and to kill a whole bunch of motherfuckers.

Chapter Nineteen

"Alpha?" Roderick interrupted Gabe from his thoughts as he stared out the window of his office. "Braxas and his people are arriving."

Gabe had a respectful working relationship with Braxas, the Alpha responsible for all of the cougar shifters in the North West, but it had been ages since he'd actually spent time with him in person. Cougars were quite different animals from wolves. He just hoped that among them all, as well as the bears who were on their way, they could learn to work together. He knew it would take a united front to defeat the Fae and their magic.

There were quite a few of his wolves standing outside when he walked off the porch and out to meet the man getting out of the expensive SUV. Wolves were rather simple creatures by nature. They lived well here, but as long as they had shelter, food, and clothes for everyone, they were pretty happy. But these cats, good lord, it looked like some sort of celebrity entourage as the line of expensive trucks came to a stop in their yard. As they began to file out of their vehicles, Gabe was suddenly very aware of *how* low maintenance most of his wolves were. It was like someone sent out a casting call for blond, muscular, golden models and Braxas's warriors were the result. Gabe knew from experience, though, that when you riled a cat you'd better be ready to deal with more than a pretty face and an expensive pair of sunglasses. These shifters were some of the stealthiest assassins in the entire shifter world. If you pissed off a wolf, he was most likely going to come right at you, but if you pissed off a cat … well, you'd better watch your ass because most of the time they attacked when you least expected it.

"Gabe," the golden haired man said as he stepped up and offered his hand. "Nice to see you again. Though I'm sorry it had to be under these types of circumstances."

"I really appreciate you standing with us for this, Braxas. Booker should be here in an hour or so, and then we'll have to move quickly to keep the element of surprise."

When a beautiful woman came to stand next to Braxas and nodded at him, Gabe just assumed that she was his mate. She was a stunning example of feminine strength and grace, with her long blonde hair and dark golden eyes drawing the attention of more than a few of his male pack members.

"Gabe, this is my second, Katrina." Braxas motioned to the woman standing next to him.

"Alpha," she purred in a low silky voice, causing Roderick to growl embarrassingly beside him. Gabe had to give the man a quick elbow and a pointed look, commanding him to calm down.

"Roderick, why don't you take Katrina and get the rest of their people settled while I catch Braxas up on what's happening with Alefric?"

Gabe led Braxas into his office. "Is it true that Booker is bringing over one hundred bears with him?" Braxas asked as Gabe poured them both a drink. "Where on earth are you going to put that much bear?"

"It's true," Gabe laughed, grateful that Braxas joked to break the tension hanging in the air. "This property was originally a hunting lodge when we purchased it. There are a couple of huge bunkhouses out back that we've refurbished. I assure you there's plenty of room, even for them."

Braxas became serious then. "So, tell me, old friend, who is this Alefric who means to enslave us?

What prompted all of this?"

Gabe wasn't sure where to start with the explanation, after all, Corrine had known this confrontation had been brewing for years now. While she'd hinted to Gabe that he'd have to be ready, it wasn't until she found out that Erica was still alive that she'd seen the battle looming ahead of them.

"Alefric is the traitor who killed the rightful King and Queen of the Elven court. He waited for their surviving daughter to come of age before he took her by force to solidify his rule, but when she reached her twenty-first birthday, she escaped. A few days ago, two of my Enforcers found her."

Braxas listened intently, apparently fascinated by what Gabe had been telling him. Shifters had very little information about the Fae, after all.

"The princess turned out to be their fated mate," Gabe continued to explain, "and that is what has cemented our involvement. Though to be honest, we're blessed that Erica did happen to stumble into her mates. Alefric has no tolerance for any race save his own, and this war would have been much worse had we not seen it coming."

"We're agreed on that part," Braxas said before standing and going to the window to look out at their people mingling in the yard. "This may be a wake-up call for all shifters. We keep to ourselves for the most part, but we can't forget that there are other magical beings out there who certainly don't see us as individual groups. My grandmother used to tell me stories of the Fae when I was a child. She told me that they subjugated shifters and used them as soldiers and slaves thousands of years ago. I always thought she was just crazy in her old age."

"I had no idea." Gabe was shocked. He knew that

to be Alefric's plan, but the fact that there had been some deranged lunatic who had actually succeeded, proved daunting to him. Even Corrine hadn't shared that information with him. But if he knew her, she would have been ashamed that her race had done something so abhorrent.

"I don't know about you, but I would rather die fighting for our freedom than become the slave to any Fae," Braxas spat out in rage.

"I agree with you, cat," a low booming voice chimed in. "When do we start?"

Gabe and Braxas both looked up in surprise to see the mountain of a man standing in the doorway to his office. The bear Alpha had arrived.

"Booker, you're early!" Gabe walked over and shook the ridiculously huge man's hand.

"We were motivated to get here quickly, and for some strange reason, other passengers decided that they would rather wait for the next ferry than ride with a hundred bear-sized men in flannel," he answered with a cheeky smile. "I can't imagine why."

"Indeed, nor can I." Braxas laughed, greeting the new Alpha. "Sweet mother, you are *huge*, man!"

Braxas and Gabe were both well above average in size, but this giant almost made Gabe feel like a child standing next to him.

"We're bears," Booker said with a shrug in answer to the cat's statement.

"I assume you sent your second off with Roderick to settle your people in?" Gabe asked as he gestured for the large man to have a seat.

"Yes, Daton and Connor are coordinating with him as we speak. My bears are ready to go at your word. This Alefric bastard will regret not minding his own business on this side of the Veil."

Elena Kincaid, Maia Dylan, and Sarah Marsh

"That's the plan, my friend. That's the plan." Gabe looked at the two shifters in front of him. They would cross the Veil and bring this fight straight to the bastard who tried to intimidate his people. Shifters may have once been enslaved, but that was a long time ago and they would never be again.

Chapter Twenty

Erica paced the eight steps that took her from one rock wall of her cell to the other, cursing Kheelan for being an ass. He had wanted to punish her for the comments she had made in the forest so rather than taking her directly to Alefric, he'd put her here in the dungeons. She fucking hated this place. It was dark, eerie and—*Sweet gods what in the hell is that stench?*

Realizing that she was freaking herself out, she took herself to her happy place. Closing her eyes, she calmed herself by thinking about her mates. As painful as it was to bring their handsome faces to mind, it definitely helped calm her. By now they would have come out of the sleeping death spell she had invoked within them, and she would bet money they would be tearing the earth realm apart looking for a way to get to her.

"Donovan had better get my message to my mates," Erica muttered to herself, rolling her shoulders in an attempt to relax.

"Donovan?" a trembling female voice asked, and Erica's eyes snapped open. "Do you mean Donovan Olson?"

Erica stepped to the front of her cell, staring into the darkened one in front of her. "I'm not sure what his last name is, but if I said the word *Beta*, what would that mean to you?"

Erica heard a distinctly feminine gasp followed by shuffling movements before a female appeared at the front of the darkened cell. She was slightly taller than Erica, with long, red hair that fell in a bedraggled mess down her shoulders, but her green eyes shone with excitement. "That is my Donovan's rank. His Alpha is a wolf by the name of Gabe Errikson."

Erica smiled at the woman. "That's him. He's

your mate?"

"Yes, he is, one of them, and we haven't, um, well, you know." A beguiling shade of red swept up her cheeks.

Erica laughed softly. "You haven't claimed each other. But that's okay. I knew my men were meant for me before we *you knowed*, too." The woman smiled back at her. "What is your name, and how in the hell did you end up down here?"

"My name is April, and Jason and I were taken from the earth realm and brought here. They have been torturing J-Jason." April's voice caught on her mate's name, and Erica's heart ached for her. "But they aren't even asking him any questions. Who the hell does that? Interrogates a man without actually asking any questions?"

Jason was a wolf shifter. Alefric and Kheelan saw them as less than Fae. Hell, they probably saw them as being less than any other being, and as Jason was a shifter, they weren't interrogating him. They were simply enjoying beating the shit out of him.

The bastards!

"Is he here with you?" Erica peered into the darkness behind the young woman.

"No, they have him on the other side of the wall." April's voice shook even more, and Erica got the impression she was desperately trying not to cry. "I hear him shouting and growling, but they won't let me see him."

Thinking about how that must feel, Erica held her hand out toward April, waiting until she reached out and they were able to clasp hands. When their hands finally touched, Erica saw a spark of blue light arc between their palms. The sensation was not exactly unpleasant, but definitely strange, and they both pulled their hands back with a gasp. The two women looked up at each other with wide eyes.

"You are a healer?" Erica whispered in shock.

April frowned in confusion, surprise clear on her face as she stared at her own palm. "I don't kn—"

Whatever April had been about to say was interrupted by the door at the end of the hall slamming open.

"Get back," Erica ordered quietly and watched as April immediately faded into the darkest corner of her cell. Erica leaned her arms out of the bars and tried her best to appear bored and disinterested.

Kheelan strode up to her cell, moving to stand directly in front of her with a smug ass look on his face. "Our King will speak with you now."

Erica stepped back from the bars. "Well as it happens, I'm just as anxious to talk with him." Kheelan opened the door, and Erica strode out. When she reached him, he held out a set of restraints. "If you think I am going to allow you to shackle me, you are crazier than I ever gave you credit for." She knew all too well that those would not be any ordinary shackles—they'd block her powers.

Kheelan's eyes narrowed. "This is standard when a prisoner is brought before our King."

"I am unarmed and outnumbered. Surely I am no threat to you or *your* King." Erica's spat the last word out with distaste. She was trying to be polite and seem as harmless as possible, but she just wasn't that good of an actress. "I will walk quietly and calmly to the throne room and speak civilly with Alefric. You have my word, but if you try to get me into those shackles, I will show you the true definition of pissed off, and you will not take me to Alefric with all the limbs you currently have attached."

Kheelan's eyes glittered red, a sign that he was losing his cool demeanor, but in all fairness, Erica didn't give a shit. She watched as Kheelan fought an internal battle, no doubt weighing up the damage that would be done if they had to fight over the shackles.

"No shackles," Kheelan grunted, then pushed her roughly in the direction of the door. Erica stumbled slightly and she heard a slight growl from the darkness to her left. Catching herself before she fell completely, she winked in April's direction. Erica put her shoulders back, held her head high and walked out the door, turning left without being told where to go, and headed for the throne room.

This was her home. She didn't need anyone telling her how to find places within these walls. As she walked the halls then began climbing the stairs that would take her directly to where Alefric was no doubt sitting on her father's throne, waiting for her to come to him, an odd calmness fell over her. Erica had thought that she might have been filled with tension or nerves in this moment. But she felt nothing but calm and determination.

With no hesitation, she followed Kheelan into the throne room and walked the long length of the room toward Alefric. The fucker sat in her father's chair, but she still remained calm and collected. When they reached the stairs that led to where Alefric was sitting, Kheelan stopped. Erica refused to stand behind the man, so she moved so that she stood half a foot in front of him, ignoring his indignant growl, and his hand gripped her upper arm.

She flung Kheelan's hand from her arm and turned to glare at him. "Touch me again, and you will pull back a bloody stump. If you think I am kidding, try me."

Kheelan bared his teeth at her and moved his hand as if to backhand her, but Erica refused to drop her gaze or raise a hand to defend herself.

"Kheelan, is that any way to welcome a guest to my home?" Alefric's asked in a voice filled with arrogance that had Erica's skin crawling. "Step back and let me talk with Eyrica."

Erica remained staring at Kheelan until he stepped back, and only then did she turn her gaze to Alefric, the False King. "I find it amusing that you and Kheelan both suffer from the same delusion. He thinks that just by saying something belongs to him that it makes it true, and it would appear you think the same. *I* am the true heir to this throne and this realm, and you are nothing."

Alefric's eyes narrowed at her. "And yet I am the one sitting on the throne with the kingdom before me, the entire proud nation of the Fae looking to me as their King."

Erica folded her arms across her chest. "Kheelan, his guards, and a few bigoted Fae stuck in the past do not make the entire Fae nation. I think you will find that there are many who see you for what you really are."

Alefric sat back on the throne, his hands gripping the armrests tightly. "And dare I ask what that might be?"

Erica sneered at the man, letting all the hatred she had for him show on her face. "A murdering egotistical asshole with delusions of grandeur. You are a prejudiced son of a bitch who thinks he has the right to slam his thoughts and beliefs down the throats of every Fae in this or any other realm. You, Alefric, are the False King. I know that if you continue to remain the False King, *my* people, the ones who have not bowed to your insanity and still hold true to their beliefs and the beliefs of their true royal family, will stand against you. They will fight with everything within them until you and every one of your fucked up followers are dead."

Alefric moved to lean forward in his chair, an insane rage shining in his eyes. "If I remain? *If*? Look around you, *Princess*. This palace is surrounded by my guards, this room is filled with the men who follow me and would die to protect their King. Their *true* King. Me! What in the hell can get to me through all of that?"

Erica reached for every fiber of strength within her, sending her love to her mates, praying that she would be able to hold them in her arms again, and know once again what it felt like to stand pressed between them, completely surrounded by their love.

Erica took one final deep breath. "Me."

Then she released her powers.

Chapter Twenty-One

All hell was breaking loose. Ben and Leo had just snuck into the castle and separated from Donovan when it felt as if an earthquake had hit, powerful enough to nearly knock them off of their feet, the magnitude sufficient enough to make the stone walls of the hallway shake in protest.

"Since when do Fae realms experience earthquakes?" Ben shouted over the fray as he and Leo stood bracing themselves in an archway. And then something dawned on him. He exchanged a look with Leo. "Erica," they said in unison.

"What the hell does she think she's doing?" Leo yelled. "She's not strong enough to hold this for long."

Ben agreed. They had no idea what Erica's plans were, but there was no way she could defeat Alefric and his guards on her own, not without some crazy and dangerous plan. He had a sinking feeling that if he and Leo didn't get to her soon and the cavalry failed to arrive in time, she would be lost to them forever. "We have to hurry, Leo."

Ben stepped out of the archway, holding on to the shaky walls for support. He ignored the thunderous sounds of protesting walls and chandeliers. His feet moved, keeping him upright despite his near lack of balance. Leo struggled identically right behind him.

Suddenly, alarms blared, a screeching, piercing sound. Ben had time to pull himself and Leo into a hidden alcove in the walls as guards poured out from every which direction. Ben carefully peered out. "They're heading east." The guards may have been running, but not without the same difficulties he and Leo had faced just moments ago. They both listened intently to discover that the source of the sound came from that exact direction. That was where Erica must be wreaking her havoc.

They waited until the hallway was clear before making their way over. The guards weren't that far ahead of them. As a matter of fact, if anyone of them would turn to look behind them, they would spot Ben and Leo, however, with all of the chaos currently ensuing, Ben doubted they would pay them any mind for now. He and Leo proceeded onward, but with caution. They stuck to trying to blend in with the walls while they moved as quickly as the quaking floors would allow them.

The guards probably should have done the same, Ben thought as one of the large crystal chandeliers came plummeting down from the high vaulted ceiling, landing on one of the guards. The ones who jumped out of the way in time were already picking themselves up off the floor while the rest ran on ahead, none of them paying any mind to their fallen comrade.

Ben and Leo had crouched low to the ground, successfully avoiding discovery. When they had reached the fallen guard, they could easily see that the man's skull had been crushed. Ben suddenly felt very grateful that the Fae did not turn to ash in their own realm.

They heard another loud boom up ahead. As they carefully moved closer, they discovered the source. Two guards were lying unconscious in front of two large double doors with brass handles. He and Leo watched as two more guards were thrown back on their asses after they attempted to touch the handles.

"We need to get in there," Ben whispered frantically. "She needs us." Something was definitely not right. He sensed it in his gut.

"I feel it, too," Leo agreed.

The quake had been slowly starting to subside.

Some of the guards began barking orders to fetch those with more magical powers or sacred objects to be used for breaking spells, and special tools to pry open locked doors. Most of the guards ran off in different directions. Ben and Leo crouched behind a large fallen statue when some of those guards ran back.

Six men were left standing by the door. Leo gave Ben a signal that had both men shifting partially. They took down four of the guards before they had a chance to know what hit them. The other two stared with wide eyes at Ben and Leo. Ben knew what they must have looked like to them with their sharp claws and half-crazed stares, and blood dripping from their elongated fangs. Ben and Leo snarled in unison, ready to rip apart the remaining men who stood between them and their mate—and then the two guards bolted, running off in separate directions.

"Fucking cowards," Leo half growled. "Reinforcements won't be far behind, and she's weakening."

Ben realized it, too. Though weaker than before, Erica's power still held steady, but he felt something else weakening, something inside of her. "No!" Something that may not be reversible. "Please, gods, no."

He and Leo both flew back and landed on their asses when they touched the door handles, but they shot up quickly and tried again and again … and again.

"Wait, brother." Leo placed his hand on Ben's chest to keep him from going for the door handle again.

"Leo, we can't stop. We have to keep trying." Ben realized how desperate he sounded, but they had no time to think of another plan. More guards would be arriving shortly, but it may be too late for Erica by then anyway.

"Can you feel that?" Leo asked. "I know you can. Just calm down and concentrate."

Ben did as Leo suggested, and there it was … their link. He could not only feel it but see its bright blue spark inside of him, a spark that grew weaker by the moment. "I see it."

"Grab on to it."

When he did, when they both did, they placed their hands—one on each door handle—and pushed the door open easily this time. Ben would not let Erica use her magic to keep her mates out. Never again. He'd fight it tooth and nail now that he knew how to reach her.

"Stop … her," Ben heard Alefric say weakly.

They walked in on Kheelan writhing in pain on the floor. Alefric was on his knees in front of the throne. His skin looked ashen and pale, and he held his hand to his chest as if trying to stop his heart from jumping out of it. Erica stood several feet away from him, her hands outstretched in his direction, palms out.

"Try … again," Alefric ordered.

Before Ben or Leo had a chance to intervene, Kheelan had reached Erica and grabbed on to her arm. The room shook harder, and Kheelan was thrown back against the wall with a large thudding sound. Ben could have sworn he heard a few bones crunch. The scum Fae slithered down the wall like the snake that he was, and landed unconscious on the ground.

"Erica," Leo called her name softly. She didn't turn, but her shoulders stiffened. He pulled back his half shift to make his voice more even. Ben pulled back his as well. "Baby, please. You need to stop this."

"I can't," she said weakly. "Don't you see? It's the only way to stop him."

Guards poured into the room now that the door had been opened. Neither Ben nor Leo bothered resisting when they surrounded them. One grabbed Ben from behind and another Leo. The hold the guard had on him felt weak, however, like he was distracted. In fact, everyone in the room stood transfixed, watching the scene that unfolded before them. Alefric bowed before the True Queen, involuntarily, of course, looking frail and sickly, while Erica, though her knees looked about ready to buckle as well, stood strong and proud, exerting her power over the False King. Ben had never felt more proud or more terrified.

"Kill … them," Alefric commanded his guard referring to Ben and Leo. Then as if someone had pressed "play" on a paused scene, the room erupted into action.

Ben felt the grip of the guard behind him get stronger, but just as quickly, the grip loosened and disappeared altogether. He turned to see the cavalry arrive. Gabe and Corrine, followed by an army of wolves, cougars, and bears poured in. More of Alefric's guards entered in droves as well. The walls and floor still shook, the alarm still blared, but all Ben could think about was his pixie.

"Worry about your mate," he heard Gabe shout through the melee, as if reading his thoughts. "We've got this."

"She's killing the King!" Ben heard a guard shout out.

The guard was right. He remembered the white light he saw when Erica had healed herself in the alleyway and the power that engulfed her when she had her nightmare. This was different. The light emitting from her was a sickly looking gray with streaks of black and red, and suddenly Ben could feel it. He could actually feel what she was doing through their link.

"She's reversing her healing power," he said to Leo.

Leo nodded. He must have understood and felt it as well.

"She's drawing his life force from him," Corrine said, suddenly appearing beside them.

"And she's using her own to do it," Ben concluded. There was no doubt in his mind that she would soon kill Alefric, but Erica may not have enough life force to survive after she succeeded.

As their cavalry fought the False King's guards, with bodies slamming into walls and furniture, with growls, and the sounds of tearing flesh and crunching bones, Erica turned to look at her men. She still held her hands out toward Alefric, never once losing focus on him, but she glanced at Ben and Leo long enough to convey a goodbye through just a look.

A tear escaped, and she mouthed the words, "*I love you,*" before she turned back to finish off her target.

Chapter Twenty-Two

Leo's wolf clamored to be let loose in the middle of the carnage, but he was terrified to lose control. He needed to focus, find a way to give Erica some of his energy. The room was a mass of chaos. More than half of the shifters were fighting in their animal forms, the roars and snarls filling the air as teeth and claws did their work on the unprepared Fae soldiers. Leo had never seen so many shifters of various kinds working together, and it had a rush of pride filling him at the stand they were all taking for their futures.

He was surprised to see Corrine and his Alpha, Gabe, both fighting against their enemies using Fae swords when they had entered the room. Leo knew that Gabe would stay in his human skin for the battle. As an Alpha, he remained equally powerful no matter what form he chose to wear, but Leo had no idea how skilled he was with a blade. It seemed there were still things he didn't know about his old friend and Alpha.

When they found Erica at the front of the room, Alefric on his knees in front of her, the impact of what she was doing to the False King hit him like a freight train. She was literally using her own life force up to vanquish the darkness in her enemy. Her healing gift had never been meant to be used this way, and the goddess would not let it go without a price.

"We can't let her do this," Ben whispered as they tried to break through the force surrounding her and Alefric, but the same magic that had tried to keep them out of the throne room was pushing at them once again. "We can't lose her this way, brother."

When Corrine briefly appeared beside Leo again, slashing one of the guards about to pounce on him unsuspected, he pleaded for the woman to give him a way to keep Erica from draining all of her life force. "She's keeping us out, Corrine. What can we do?"

"Give her a reason to stay," she replied, a frightened look on her face as she gazed back on Erica.

"Erica, love." Leo placed both his hands on the barrier in front of them. When Erica turned her head in his direction, he looked into her strained, bloodshot eyes and said, "Please don't leave us. We need you. I need you."

Leo could feel both Erica's and his brother's pain through their link as they all longed for things that fate looked to take from them. Their future, their family, it all seemed to be slipping away faster than they could control. When Erica finally mouthed the words, "*forgive me*" towards them, Leo's entire universe seemed to implode. She was telling them goodbye.

Just then, they felt the flickering of the barricade lower. Erica pulled on it so hard, the force of it dropped both him and Ben farther back and onto their knees. Leo knew what she was doing. He could feel it. She was gathering her magic and going in for the kill.

Then a thought occurred to him. They were connected. He and Ben could feel her using her magic, and if they could both feed her some of their combined energy, some of their life force, together they'd be strong enough to take Alefric's life-force without any of them losing their life in the process.

He began to draw on his energy, knowing that Ben would immediately feel and understand what he was doing and follow suit. But before he had a chance to connect with Erica, he saw out of the corner of his eye, a blur of a guard's uniform lunging forward, sword extended towards their mate's back. It was that bastard Kheelan. With her current weakening state, her shield might not be strong enough to keep him out. Leo gasped. He and Ben were too far away to stop him.

"No! You won't touch her!" Corrine yelled as she stepped in front of Kheelan's sword. Everyone stopped fighting and focused on the sacrifice that had just been made.

"No! Corrine," Erica called out, dropping her hands in a moment of panic.

Corrine seemed to be the most surprised when she looked down at her chest and saw the long blade protruding from her, but then she turned her head towards the man at her back.

"I've longed to take your life since the day you took my Queen, Kheelan," she said weakly. "You are a traitor to your people and will die a traitor's death."

"It seems you are the one who will die, bitch," Kheelan sneered right before Corrine smiled back at him, causing first an expression of confusion to cross his face. Shock replaced it with her next action.

"We both will, *ud'ran*," Corrine whispered with satisfaction as she plunged her own sword right through her stomach, impaling both herself and the traitor.

Leo felt Erica's draw on their power halt abruptly as she screamed and lunged forward, reaching Corrine and Kheelan's bodies as they collapsed onto the stone floor. It was all he could do to not go to his mate. Her devastation at losing Corrine had finally been the straw that broke her, but his wolf knew that they needed to eradicate the threat before they comforted her.

"Ben," he called out to his brother, nodding towards the King who was now bending on only one knee, already beginning to recover. "Let's end this."

They both shifted into their wolves and were on Alefric in seconds. His screams as they went straight for his throat, ripping and tearing at his weakened body, only drew them further into the bloodlust. They'd end him, the False King, who thought to harm their mate, who thought to take what was theirs.

Finally, the soft sobbing of the woman they loved broke through the haze, and Leo realized that the False King was truly dead beneath them. He willed the wolf back to its cage before turning to see to his mate.

Gabe was now beside Erica. They had separated Corrine from Kheelan's lifeless body, and she looked so small lying there in their Alpha's arms.

"Please, Corrine, don't leave me. Gods, please don't leave me," Gabe pleaded frantically as he tried to stop the flow of blood from the gaping wounds in her torso and chest. Leo finally saw that there was more to the relationship between the Fae woman and his leader than the pair of them had admitted. Maybe they had yet to admit it to themselves.

Gabe's gaze lifted to their mate, the pain that swirled within his eyes almost too painful to acknowledge. "Heal her, Erica. Please."

Chapter Twenty-Three

"I don't know if I can," Erica whispered. She stared down at the broken woman who lay in the Alpha's arms. "But I will try."

For the second time, Erica drew from within herself, pulling her healing energy to the fore. She felt the warmth of her power surging through her, traveling down her arms and into her palms. She held them over Corrine and called on the gods to help her. This was not how it was supposed to end. Erica had survived the battle with Alefric. She had stood up to him and had been willing to end her own life in order to give her kingdom and her people the future they deserved.

Corrine had faced so much and given so much of herself, it seemed unfair that the gods deemed it necessary for her to be taken.

"Fuck that, and fuck them!"

Erica drew on her own life force, pulling as much of it forward as she could, feeding it to Corrine, sending her prayers and thoughts, begging her to stay with them. Gabe still cradled her against his chest. For a moment, Erica felt a responding warmth within Corrine, almost as if her spirit were reaching out toward Erica, determined to stay with them. But then it faded back into nothingness.

"No," Erica sobbed, forcing even more of herself into Corrine. Erica knew there was not a lot left within her to call upon. Fighting Alefric had almost killed her, and this … well, this might just finish the job, but she refused to pull back. If Corrine was to slip into the afterlife this night, then Erica would do everything in her power to stop that, including taking her place and making the journey for her.

No sooner had that thought formed than Erica felt

a surge of power within her. A power and strength she had never felt before. It came with a sense of protection and anger at her own thoughts, and that was enough to have it dawn on her that this newfound energy was coming from her mates. They were fighting for her and with her for Corrine. She had no clue how it was possible, but that didn't stop her from grabbing hold, harnessing their power and pushing it into Corrine.

With the additional strength, she reached for Corrine's fading spirit, pulling her from the dark and dragging her toward the light. When it seemed like an opposite power pulled Corrine back into the afterlife, Erica growled.

"Oh, hell no. She's ours!" Then with one last surge, she pulled Corrine's spirit into the light.

Erica collapsed back as she settled the healing energy back within her. She leaned heavily against her mates, who were both kneeling behind her, cradling Erica against their chests, as she desperately gasped for air. Her entire body felt heavy, and the thought of even lifting her head felt impossible.

"Erica?" Ben asked urgently, and Erica patted his knee, not quite able to form words. She blinked a few times to focus and looked down at Corrine. She was still wrapped tightly in a relieved Gabe's arms, staring right back at her. She did not look happy.

"Eyrica, what were you thinking?" Corrine's voice was barely a whisper. "You could have been killed."

Both Leo and Ben growled behind her, and Erica rolled her eyes. *"Quenya,* you could have kept that little snippet to yourself. You're going to get me in trouble."

Leo barked a laugh. "Oh hell, pixie, you were already in trouble. Did you think Ben and I wouldn't catch your purpose along our bond?"

Ben tightened his arm around her, hugging her tighter. "We knew your intention as soon as you thought it. If you'd gone over, we would have gone with you."

"I couldn't just let her die. And no way in hell would you have gone over anywhere!"

"That goes ditto for you, baby."

"You are one of the bravest people that I have ever met, and that is why you aren't in *too* much trouble," Leo growled with pride in his voice against the sensitive skin of her neck, making Erica shiver, "but we will be turning your ass red as soon as the opportunity presents itself, mate."

Erica felt goosebumps form along her skin at the heat in Leo's tone and knew it was no idle threat. But to be fair, the thought of being spanked by her mates wasn't much of a punishment. The idea thrilled her to no end.

"I gotta say," Ben began, "that's a pretty amazing power you have there—the ability to cause earthquakes."

"I had no idea I could do that."

"You tapped into something very powerful, Eyrica," Corrine said somberly. "Dark Elemental magic is both powerful and dangerous."

"April!" a man's voice roared from just beyond the entrance to the throne room, putting a halt to their discussion. Erica's startled gaze looked to the door, just as Donovan flew into the room, practically dragging a badly injured man with him. "April. Someone took her!"

"Donovan! What the hell is going on?" Gabe shouted back. As soon as Donovan saw his Alpha, he ran toward him. The man he carried moaned but moved as fast as he could. "Goddess of mercy, is that Jason? What the fuck happened to him?"

The man with Donovan must have been his brother Jason. It was difficult to see any family resemblance in the two men due to the fact that his face was a complete mess. Swollen and misshapen, blood both dried and fresh adorning his chin, it told a frightening story.

"Alpha, please," Donovan pleaded as he dropped to his knees beside them, his brother collapsing beside him. "I know I have disgraced myself in your eyes, my actions not those of the man I know I can be. But please, you have to help us. April, our mate, she is missing."

Erica gasped. "Missing? She's not in the dungeon where she was being kept?"

Donovan and Jason both turned to look at Erica, and she could see the desperation in their eyes. "No, she wasn't," Jason rasped, his voice cracking. "Just after Donovan got to me, we heard her scream. She was calling for h-help." The man's voice broke on that last word.

"Someone took her," Donovan continued for his brother. "They came into the dungeons and took her. We have to find her. Please, Alpha, help us find her."

"Why would someone in this realm want a human woman?" Corrine asked, her face a mask of confusion.

"This must have something to do with the missing humans," Leo informed. "We've been tracking so many reported cases as of late."

Erica remembered Ben and Leo telling her about this at breakfast, that for the past six months, they along with other Enforcers of their pack, had been tracking the large number of Fae entering the human realm and also the missing humans they were responsible for taking. She knew Fae traitors had been after her, but she wondered what they could possibly want with humans. April was actually not even human though, at least not fully, something the woman had apparently been clueless of herself. The question remained, who else knew of April's mixed heritage or had figured it out?

The answer that came to Erica was as impossible as it was horrifying.

"Kheelan!" Erica pushed out of her mates' arms, desperately searching the floor behind them. Corrine had run the fucker through with her blade, but had anyone stopped to check if he was actually dead? The spot where his body should have still been was empty save for a pool of blood. It looked as if someone had dragged his body away.

"Kheelan's not dead?" Corrine asked in a small tone, and Erica heard Gabe growl low. She didn't catch what the man said to Corrine, but whatever it was it had an instant calming effect.

Erica groaned as she pushed to her feet, desperately searching the carnage around her for his body, hoping that he'd only managed to crawl some distance away before succumbing to death. Her dread began to increase when there was nothing. No sign of him. No one would have bothered moving him if he were dead.

"What would he want with a human?" Leo asked as he wrapped an arm around Erica's waist.

Erica turned to look at the two men that called April mate. They both stood and stared intently at her as she spoke. "Because she is not human. She is Fae. And she is a healer."

Gasps of surprise rang around the room at Erica's revelation before everyone finally sprang into action. By the lack of surprise on Jason's face, however, he seemed much more informed. He also looked like he could use some much needed rest before recounting everything he knew and what that bastard, Kheelan had put him through. Erica was the true Queen of the Fae, and right now her duty was to clean house, to find any traitors who escaped, to punish those who had already begun to surrender, and to welcome all who had always remained loyal.

"We will find Kheelan," Erica vowed to both Donovan and Jason. "And he will be brought to justice." She just hoped they would be in time to save April, discover what had been done to the other humans, and why they were taken in the first place.

Chapter Twenty-Four

Ben had had enough. He watched as Erica immediately took up her diplomatic role, speaking with the packs, trying to both comfort them and thank them for their aid. There were wounded on both sides, but fortunately not many of the shifters had perished. Erica looked dead on her feet and still very weak from nearly having the life force drained out of her. When she almost stumbled trying to get to one of the injured bear shifters, Ben intercepted her.

"You're getting some rest ... now!" he commanded.

There would be plenty of time for her to take on her new role as Queen, and he and Leo as Kings, apparently. He already knew that this would be what had to happen somewhere in the back of his mind, but the full force of it had just hit him. He and Leo briefly discussed their new roles, and Gabe had reassured them that even though they would no longer be Enforcers, they, along with Erica, were forever part of the pack and would still be privy to all pack matters.

Big changes were coming, that much was definitely clear. The packs would be working alongside the Fae now to keep the peace among both realms, but without the big threat hanging over them, they had time to figure things out.

Taking care of Erica was his and Leo's top priority now. Erica didn't protest when they led her out of the battle room and away from all of the carnage. And she didn't protest when Ben lifted her in his arms in a cradled position when they reached a flight of stairs, Leo beside them, and carried her up. She directed him past several rooms before instructing him to stop at one of the alcoves, where she revealed a secret passageway.

"I don't think that these rooms have been tainted by Alefric or his followers," she said when at the end of the passageway they came upon four rooms. Erica explained that these rooms were built in case they were ever under attack. The royal family and their staff could hide here for a while and escape to the outside when the coast was clear.

"When I was a child, I used to play in these rooms." She laughed quietly as she thought back. "My parents never knew that I would bring some of my forest folk friends here to have tea parties and play. Those were happy times."

"We have a lifetime of happy memories ahead of us to give you, love," Leo promised, and Ben agreed.

Ben carried Erica over the threshold of one of the rooms before gently placing her down on her feet and taking in all of the surroundings. Strange that a room that had sat empty and secret for so many years looked vibrant and lived in. No dust on any of the dark cherry furniture. The bright blue curtains and matching bedspreads looked as if they had been laundered, the bed freshly made, and the pillows fluffed. Ben vowed to himself to make an effort to understand how the magic in this realm worked.

"Let's get you cleaned up," Leo suggested, and the three of them began toeing off their shoes and shedding their clothes along the way to the en-suite bathroom.

Ben was in awe when he stepped into the large room. The toilet and sink looked like the kind they had in the human realm, but the large stone tub in the center of the room looked like hot springs you'd find among the wooded wilds. He turned on the brass faucet and watched as the tub filled in minutes, steaming and bubbling as it did. The bottom of the tub felt soft against his feet when he stepped in, like moss at the bottom of a lake.

But what awed him the most was the brave woman now sitting snuggled in between him and Leo. They could have lost her today and missed out on all the wonderful years that lay ahead of them. He was beyond grateful that they hadn't.

"You will never do that to us again, Erica." Leo tried to be firm, but instead, he almost choked on the words.

"I'm so sorry that I hurt you both," she said looking from one to the other. Ben knew her words rang true. Being separated from them, thinking she would never see them again no doubt cost her as much as it did them. "And, well … the whole sleeping death thing … maybe we could just overlook that one?" she added sheepishly.

"Oh, no, no, pixie," Ben tsked. "You can bet your red bottom we won't be overlooking that one." He couldn't help but laugh at the deer in the headlights look she gave him.

"Something tells me you'll enjoy a good spanking," Leo winked at Erica, "but for tonight, let us just take care of you."

Ben watched as Leo pulled their pixie in close for a passionate kiss, and he followed suit as soon as Leo had released her. By the time their kiss ended, all three of them were panting heavily. They needed to slow things down a little. Although Erica's strength was quickly returning, largely due to the fact that Leo and Ben had fed her some more of their energy, she needed all of her strength for what they had planned for her. If she was up to it, they would take her together tonight, solidifying their mating bond.

"Oh, I am up for it," Erica replied seductively

when Ben told her of their plans. "I want you both so much. Please, make me yours fully."

The three of them quickly bathed, washing away any trace of the earlier battle and any debris left over from the massive quake Erica had produced. Ben had her giggling when he informed her of a different way she would feel the Earth move tonight.

At first, Leo had insisted that Erica get some rest beforehand and Ben had to agree, but when she adamantly protested against it, Ben knew he could no longer keep from touching her.

He stepped out of the hot springs tub taking Erica with him. Leo grabbed them each an oversized fluffy towel from the cabinet above the toilet. They both dried Erica off first, despite her protests that she could do it herself.

"Where's the fun in that, love?"

When they were dry, Leo hoisted Erica up into his arms, and she eagerly straddled his hips as he carried her into the bedroom. He then gently placed her in the middle of the bed. Ben soaked in her naked body with ravenous eyes, trying to calm the wolf within. They needed to go slow, although, in truth, he wanted to as well. He wanted to savor this moment, the moment they first took her together, and forever burn it into his memory.

Patience, wolf. She'll be fully ours tonight.

Chapter Twenty-Five

"Hmm, brother," Leo teased as he admired the dewy glow of their mate fresh from the bath. "How should we take our sweet pixie this first time? Should we fuck her sweet and slow on our sides?"

He loved the way Erica whimpered and her hands moved up to cup and caress her breasts, making Ben growl low next to him.

"Ben, why don't you help our mate with those luscious breasts? While I have a taste of her delicious little pussy?" Leo slowly climbed onto the bed at her feet, moving his hands up her long legs. "Mmm, baby, I can smell your sweetness already, and it's making my mouth water."

Erica gasped as Ben moved beside her and took her wrists in one hand, binding them above her head, and then he dove in and began to worship her perfect breasts with his tongue and lips.

"Goddess, yes," Erica moaned as Leo's hands finally reached her hips and he settled himself in between her legs, leaning in to nuzzle at the junction of her thighs.

Damn, how did Ben and I end up so blessed as to have Erica for our mate? Leo was astonished at how beautiful, smart, and incredibly strong she was, not to mention humbled that she'd accepted them at her side.

Leo took his time, spreading her glistening folds wide to reveal the bounty within. She was soaking already, and he couldn't resist any longer. He slid a hand under her and lifted her just enough to lick her little rosebud and then all the way back up to focus on the swollen button of flesh at the top. When he wrapped his lips around her clit and sucked hard, Erica's hips bucked up in his hold.

"Leo!" she screamed as he sank two fingers into

her pussy and began to slowly draw them in and out, still teasing her nub with his teeth.

Leo looked up to see Ben lifting his head to capture her mouth in a rough, dominating kiss before he went back to his feast. Leo was determined to see their mate scream out her pleasure before he sank himself deep inside of her pussy as his brother took her ass. Just imagining how good it would feel had the pre-cum seeping from his cock. Leo could think of nowhere he would rather be than inside of his mate.

"Are you ready for a little more, baby?" he asked as he took his other hand and gently fingered her puckered hole, using the wetness from her own body to ease its way inside.

"Mmm, whatever that was that you did, brother," Ben chuckled in between kisses along her neck and back down to her hard nipples, "do it again. Our mate's eyes just rolled back into her head."

"Yes, that feels amazing," Erica moaned as Leo continued to finger-fuck her ass while still eating away at her pussy. "Oh God, I think I'm going to…"

Leo thrust three fingers into her wet sheath as he stilled the one in her ass and pulled hard on her clit with his lips, loving the squeal that came out of her mouth as her entire body bowed up off the bed. He could feel her muscles contracting around his fingers, and he couldn't wait to feel it when he buried his cock balls deep inside of her.

****

Erica moaned into Ben's mouth while her body shook from her orgasm. Ben continued kissing her as she rode out the last remnants of it.

"Isn't she so fucking beautiful when she comes for us?" Leo asked, still sitting between her legs.

Ben murmured his agreement after finally releasing her lips. "I need a little taste, too." He sat up on his haunches and leaned over to taste her glistening wet pussy, Leo having just vacated the spot for him.

Erica meanwhile took his rigid cock in one of her small hands and began stroking him slowly. He moaned against her pussy lips, causing her to grip him tighter. He heard his brother groaning as well and stopped his ministrations briefly to look up and see that Erica had her lips wrapped around his brother's cock.

"That is so fucking hot!"

Erica released Leo's cock with a loud pop and turned to Ben. "I need to taste you, too." Who was he to argue?

He took one last swipe, savoring her delicious flavor on his tongue before he sat back up and moved closer to Erica's mouth. She laved her tongue around his mushroomed head, teasing him before sucking his tip into her mouth. Then she licked again and again, torturing him some more while stroking Leo's cock.

She switched it up again, taking Leo into her mouth while stroking Ben. It all became too much by the time his turn to be in her mouth rolled around again. Her eyes closed when she took him deep, her moans of pleasure indicated that she got off on his flavor as much as he got off on hers. He tilted his head back and closed his eyes, but the images of her sucking him and then his brother, her plump lips and hollowed cheeks, were still visible in his mind.

As good as her lips and tongue felt around his cock, he desperately needed to be inside of her. "Stop, baby. Fuck … I need to be inside you now." He felt his canines lengthen with the need to bite, to mark his mate again. His wolf would not be denied now.

Leo seemed just as desperate. His brother shifted

on the bed, positioning himself on his back and in one swift move, he flipped Erica on top of him. Erica straddled him, grinding herself against Leo while she kissed him.

Leo spread his legs wide enough to make room for Ben and wrapped his arms around Erica. Ben took his place behind Erica, marveling at the sexy sight before him. Her ass and pussy were exposed to him, ready and waiting to be filled by her men.

He swiped two fingers between her glistening wet folds and then inserted them into her little rosebud, eliciting a long and desperate sounding moan from Erica. He stroked inside of her with his fingers a few times more before determining that she was definitely ready.

He removed his fingers. "We're going to make you feel so good, pixie."

"Mmmm."

Leo lifted her hips and entered Erica to the hilt. Then Ben very slowly pushed his way in until he, too, was completely buried inside of her. They all froze for a moment, the other two seeming to relish finally being so connected just as much as he did.

When the tightness of holding still overwhelmed him, he began to move. Nice long strokes, alternating in and out with his brother. Ben had no idea what Heaven felt like, but he imagined that this probably came pretty damn close.

****

Erica's eyes grew heavy as she held herself still. Her mates were moving in and out of her in a syncopated rhythm that was clearly designed to drive her crazy. She had never felt so full, so needy, so damned pleasured in all her life. Taking two deep breaths she bore down on her orgasm, not wanting this to end. Having both her mates buried to the hilt within her was the most amazing feeling in the world. When she finally succumbed to the pleasure building within her, she wanted to make sure she took her mates with her.

A small revolution of her hips as both men pushed within her had both Ben and Leo groaning.

"Fuck, mate," Leo growled from beneath her, his hands clenching hard against her hips, "do that again." Erica bit her bottom lip at the need in his tone and swirled her hips again. This time, her mates' rhythm faltered.

"Too much!" Ben's voice sounded garbled, a sure sign his wolf was close. "Fuck, I can't control—" And then he began to slam into her. The movement and force of his hips crashing into hers drove her into Leo, sparking an instant reaction from him. Erica clenched her hands into the bed sheets below them as Leo and Ben began to pound into her, driving her closer and closer to the edge of insanity that came with the pleasure only they could build within her. Erica keened as the size of her approaching orgasm felt life-altering.

"Come for us, Erica," Leo groaned. "Gods, please come."

"Go over, our Queen," Ben added in a growl. "Take us with you."

And that was all it took. Erica hovered on the edge for a split second before she tumbled with a scream in the maelstrom of pleasure she had held at bay. Her orgasm crashed within her, making her jerk and thrash between her mates. Both men roared their own pleasure to the room, moments before she felt their simultaneous bites against the sensitive skin of her neck. Right over the claiming marks that already existed, and as impossible as it had seemed just moments before, she peaked again, screaming their names to the gods.

"Mmm." Erica moaned what felt like only moments later, as she lifted her head to look at the man beneath her. She had to blink a few times to clear her vision and bring Leo into focus. The power of her release was such that her head still spun.

"There's my love," Leo murmured as he leaned up and pressed a sweet kiss to her lips.

Erica stretched a little, enjoying the slight pinch within her that told her she had been well loved. "That's me," she replied, her voice raspy from all the screaming she had been doing. The bed moved as Ben lay down beside them, and Erica turned to him with a frown. "How did you get over there?"

Ben grinned, his face devoid of stress or fear for the first time that day. "Well, my Queen, you passed out. I went to run us another bath. We took you hard, and the hot water will feel good."

Erica nodded and rested her chin on her hand over Leo's heart, and reached out her hand to Ben. When he lifted it and pressed a kiss to the back of it before settling it against his own heart she sighed. If anyone were to ever ask her what it was to be mated, to be claimed by two wolves who owned her heart and soul, she would never be able to put it into words. But the memory of this moment would most definitely be the one that came to mind.

Erica let out a contented sigh. "I need to thank you both for coming over the bridge and beyond the Veil for me."

Leo frowned up at her and tensed slightly beneath her. "Erica, don't thank us for doing what we were born to do. We will always come for you, and nothing will ever come between us."

"And don't think apologizing gets you out of that

punishment we talked about," Ben added with a devilish grin. "I think all three of us are looking forward to that."

Erica grinned back. "I think you might be right. But the fact that you came after me means more than you will ever truly know."

Leo nodded toward the door with his head, and Ben rolled off the bed, heading toward the bathroom. Leo stood up and, in a testament to his strength, simply lifted her with him. He slid his hands beneath her bottom, and she wrapped her legs around his hips. She moaned as his first step had her still sensitive clit rubbing against his hard abdomen.

"We weren't just coming after you, baby," Leo murmured as he carried her into the bathroom. "We were chasing fate."

****

"When one abuses a trust, there is always a penalty."

Erica gasped for breath as she sat bolt upright in the bed, the final words of her goddess still ringing in her ears and her heart pounding hard within her chest.

"Erica?" Leo asked from beside her, leaning up to stare into her face. The room was dark, but the light of the moon outside the window cast an eerie light within the room, making it possible for her to see the concern on Leo's face.

Ben wrapped an arm around her from his position on her right, surrounding her in warmth she could not feel. "What is it, love? Bad dream?"

Unable to find her voice, she simply nodded. She had known that there would be a penance to pay for what she did. She was a healer, a Fae blessed by the goddess with a gift so precious it should never have been used for anything other than good. But this? Oh gods, this she had never imagined. She'd believed the penance would be hers and hers alone to pay, but to have her mates punished at the same time, that she had not foreseen.

"Come here, baby," Ben murmured as he drew her tight against his chest and lay back down. "Damn, Erica, you're shaking."

Leo lay down close behind her. "Must have been one hell of a nightmare. You wanna talk about it?"

Erica shook her head. She couldn't bring herself to tell them. Not yet. She wrapped an arm around Ben and curled her leg back over Leo's wanting to be as close to her mates as possible. She tried to quiet her mind enough to rest, but it was impossible. Leo and Ben had chased fate to come for her, but it looked like Fate would have the last word.

Erica could only hope that it was one the three of them could live with.

Epilogue

Erica sat in the throne room, listening half-heartedly to one of the elders read through the coronation scriptures that would, when finished, announce her as Queen of the Fae. She looked around at all those who had come to celebrate this day with her. Before her stood her people, the Fae who always remained loyal to the true royal family, never wavering beneath the rule of the False King. Amongst them were the shifters, all of those she remembered from the day Alefric had turned her throne room into a battleground two weeks ago, and many she had yet to meet.

But meet them she would. Every single one of them had risked their lives to travel to the Elf realm and fight against Alefric and his reign of terror. She had so many people to thank, and she would make it her mission to let them know how much they meant to her.

As her gaze passed over the crowd she locked eyes with the tall man with short dark hair cropped close to his head, leaning against the back wall. Donovan stood with his arms crossed over his large chest, the tribal tattoo visible on his forearm. Jason stood beside him, just as tall, but his expression was a lot harder, and Erica could understand why. Alefric had tortured him physically, but it was the mental torture of knowing his mate had been just on the other side of the wall and beyond his reach to help, that was the true torment he had to live with now.

They nodded in her direction, and she returned the gesture with a small smile. Her heart ached for Donovan and his brother. After the battle was over, Erica had tried to help Jason heal the wounds that Kheelan had carved into his flesh, but it seemed as though his own body was fighting the process. She could not understand why it wouldn't work. The goddess had a plan. Erica kept on reminding herself of that. She still hadn't been able to bring herself to share with her mates what the ultimate cost of using her powers to defeat Alefric had been. It was still too painful to admit even to herself, the price that all three of them would be paying in the end, not just Erica. There were other important matters to attend to now, however. So far their search for April and the other humans had gotten them all nowhere. Erica couldn't even begin to imagine the frustration and pain they were going through.

"Baby," Leo murmured quietly, leaning toward her from the throne he sat on to her left, "this is supposed to be the day you take back your birthright. So why the sad face?"

Erica sighed. "April." *And the horrible secret I am keeping from you for now, my loves.*

Both her mates reached over the elaborately carved arms of the throne she sat on and took a hand each, the gentle stroke of their thumbs against her skin and squeeze of their hands giving her comfort.

"We'll find her," Ben promised. "Our pack-mates need their mate. Even if it takes every shifter we have to search every inch of this realm and ours to find her, then that is what we will do."

"Corrine!" Gabe's voice echoed through the throne room, bringing an abrupt halt to the ceremony. Erica and her mates stood quickly and walked down the stairs of the dais to where Corrine had collapsed against Gabe. From her pale expression and shallow breath, Erica knew Corrine was experiencing another vision.

The elder stepped over to her and grabbed her arm. "Your Majesty, we must—"

"Take your hand off my mate," Leo growled, "or

I will rip it off your body."

Erica pressed a hand against Leo's chest, calming the man as well as the wolf. "Just wait, Calanon. We can finish in a moment."

Corrine inhaled sharply just moments before her eyes fluttered open. "He brings her powers forward. He is fighting a strong magic that has hidden her abilities for many years, but he is forcing his way through the shields. She's scared, and in pain, but fighting him in her own way."

There was movement beyond their group and bursts of outrage that were quickly silenced. Then Donovan and Jason stepped out of the crowd.

"She who?" Jason growled his voice more wolf than man.

Corrine turned to look at them, sadness shimmering in her eyes. "Your mate."

A roar of rage, which morphed quickly into the anguished howl of Jason's wolf, as he shifted, exploded from him.

"Jason!" Gabe yelled, the air in the room suddenly thickening. Erica knew it was the essence of an Alpha looking to reach one of his pack. "You will calm yourself, and you will stay in this room."

The large wolf paced, growling constantly, obeying, but making it clear to everyone in the room that he wasn't happy about it.

"Where is she?" Donovan asked Corrine in an anguished voice.

Corrine reached out a hand and placed it on Donovan's arm. "If I knew, we would already be on our way, young wolf, but I do not know. All I can tell you is that you and your brother will play a role in helping her. You all have a long way to go before deciding her fate."

"Majesty, I must insist," Calanon started, but

Erica reached out and clamped her hand over his mouth, and spun to face him.

"Shut up!" Erica snapped, her eyes blazing. "We have things to do and a fucking Fae healer to find. I am now Queen, correct?" Calanon nodded, his eyes wide. "The council and all Fae will recognize the mates deemed mine by the Fates and by the claiming bites we wear, right?" Again, Calanon nodded. "Then this coronation is over, and we enter the rescue planning phase of the day."

Erica pushed the man away.

"Damn, baby," Leo drawled, "I love it when you get all Queenly and dominant."

Erica laughed. "Good to know."

"It works here, and with everyone else," Ben added in whisper for their ears only as he stepped in and wrapped an arm around her. "But not with us. Just remember that and we won't have to punish you. Again."

Erica nodded with a grin, recalling the punishments she'd experienced at the hands of her mates. Their hands had done magical things that made her shiver all over again just thinking about them.

"Fair enough, but for now, there is a healer out there who needs our help," Erica said. Then she addressed the people within the throne room, lifting her voice to be heard clearly all the way to the back. "We have taken back our palace, and we have defeated the mad bastard who thought to take away our free will, but there is more to be done. We must bring all of Alefric's supporters to justice and hold them accountable for the atrocities they have committed."

Murmurs of agreement and excitement began to fill the room.

"And we must start with Kheelan. We must find

him, and save the Fae healer he has taken with him. And we must find and hopefully return the other humans he has kidnapped. This is not only the right thing to do, but it is our goddamn obligation!"

The crowd roared in agreement. Erica took a deep breath, satisfied that her parents would be proud of the woman she had become.

She was Eyrica, a healer among her people, Queen of the Fae, and mate to Leo and Ben Eklund. It was her role in life to protect her people and punish anyone who thought to hurt them. Starting with delivering April safely to her mates. The fact that she would get to wreak justice on Kheelan was just an added benefit.

A benefit that she was going to enjoy the ever loving hell out of.

The End

Elena Kincaid, Maia Dylan, and Sarah Marsh

EVERNIGHT PUBLISHING ®

www.evernightpublishing.com